THE BRITISH BILLIONAIRE

A BEAUTY & THE BEAST RETELLING

BRITNEY M. MILLS

CRYSTAL CANYON PUBLISHING

To Karen O'Connor and Rebecca Andrew

For helping me get all the bits and bobs right in this book.

CHAPTER 1

*P*acing back and forth behind the bus stop enclosure, Isabelle Rousseau dialed her sister, Juliette. It had been one of those awful weeks where even with her best efforts, she'd failed. The stifling mid-July air of the London afternoon didn't help her spirits either.

Her sister answered after the second ring. "Hey, sis. How are you?" Isabelle could hear papers shuffling in the background, meaning Juliette was still at work.

Pulling the phone back to look at the time, Isabelle realized it was only two in the afternoon. She'd put off this call long enough, and she hoped her sister could at least hear her out before offering some perfect answer Isabelle should have been thinking about before.

"Do you have a minute?" she tried to say as calmly as possible, fighting to keep the tears at bay and her voice stronger than she felt. Juliette was dedicated to the skin care company she'd started a few years before, and even though she was only two years older, sometimes Isabelle felt like it was more like five. At twenty-five, Isabelle hadn't quite "made it," still working as an assistant to an interior designer.

As happy as she was for Juliette's success, there were still times a shot of envy reared its head.

"Rough day with Darcy?" Juliette paused, and Isabelle kept silent, not ready to say anything about her boss, knowing it would only add ammo to the fire. "I don't know why you continue to work for her."

Twisting a lock of her dark brown hair around one finger, Isabelle stared at the ground as she paced, her annoyance easing somewhat as she had someone to vent to.

"I know. You say this every time I have a rough day, but I need this job. Darcy Stewart is the best interior designer and stager in London. With her approval, I can get any job I want just from sticking it out." Isabelle sucked in a breath, waiting for her sister's response.

"But for how long, Isa? If you don't stand up to her now, how are you going to do it five years down the road when you have another job offer? I think you're too comfortable."

"*Too comfortable?*" she shouted and paused as several heads snapped in her direction. With the adrenaline pumping through her now, she lowered her voice and said, "There is no way I'm too comfortable. I think she's giving me an ulcer."

Juliette chuckled. "You always were a little dramatic. Maybe you should take a vacation. You haven't had one of those in the three years you've worked for her."

Isabelle frowned and stopped walking. A vacation sounded wonderful. But she knew it would only end in having to field Darcy's phone calls at all hours.

"I just wish there was a way to be a stager for myself. Everyone around here needs a million recommendations, but I don't have a name established within the industry."

"That isn't the worst thing in the world. You've got some savings. Do the math. How long can you go without a paycheck to tide you over? Do as much as you can to prepare for your business, make a business plan, and then give your notice. I can have Tristan help you with a marketing plan." Isabelle could picture her sister's face, matter-of-fact and no-nonsense.

As much as she appreciated the help, she wasn't sure she wanted her sister's fiancé to help her. He was a nice enough guy, but she couldn't help but feel intimidated when he was around. Although, she'd only met him once when she'd gone back home at the beginning of the month. Tristan had come with Juliette that weekend to set up something else for her parents' business. They were the perfect match, billionaire marketing exec and self-starter skin care guru.

Isabelle rolled her eyes. Things like the perfect man coming into her life didn't happen to Isabelle.

"I didn't call to talk about work or what my five-year plan should look like." Isabelle closed her eyes, leaning against the building nearest the stop. Putting a hand on her forehead, she said, "Aaron broke up with me. Two nights ago."

Silence permeated through the phone, and Juliette's voice was softer when she spoke. "I'm so sorry, Isabelle. Did he give you a reason why?"

A tear rolled down her cheek, and she took a few extra seconds to compose herself. "I'm not good enough for him."

"Please tell me he didn't say that. If he did, he's more of an idiot than I expected."

Isabelle's jaw dropped. "What do you mean, 'idiot'? You just met him three weeks ago, and you said he was nice."

"Nice? You thought that's what I'd say to give my approval for your fiancé?" Juliette's words called up a familiar image in Isabelle's head, the look Juliette had perfected over the course of her lifetime. Her eyes took on a bored expression while she pursed her lips, looking displeased.

Shaking her head, Isabelle said, "Why didn't you come out and say it, then? It would have saved me time." She was near shouting now and turned to face away from the other people waiting in the area.

"Would you have listened? You looked pretty smitten to me."

"Probably not."

Juliette sniffed. "Tell me what happened."

Isabelle thought about the night she'd gone out with Aaron, how excited she'd been to try the new restaurant that had opened in London. He was from a very well-to-do family, and there had been several perks over the course of their six-month relationship. But she should have listened to her gut after meeting his parents two weeks earlier. Things hadn't gone well, and her more humble upbringing was called into question.

"He picked me up, and instead of going to dinner like we'd planned, the driver drove down a few streets and stopped. Aaron turned to me and said, 'This isn't going to work out. If I'm going to make it to Parliament, I need someone who understands business just as much as I do. You're beautiful, but all this design stuff will get you nowhere.'"

"Do you believe him?"

The question stunned Isabelle, and she didn't move for a moment, reconsidering her words.

"Yes."

"About which part?" Why did Juliette have to be so annoying when she was right?

"About all of it. His parents looked at me like the gum stuck to the bottom of their shoes. I wasn't after their money. I just thought I loved their son. Turns out he didn't feel the same."

She wiped at the tears flowing freely now. Taking a sip from the takeout cup of tea she held, she turned to look for the bus. When her sister didn't say anything, she said, "And I really don't know much about business anyway."

"You can, though. You've got the head for it. And the parts you don't know or don't want to deal with, you hire out. Isabelle, I'm serious. You have a great eye for design. I come into my office every day since you've decorated it and have to smile because it's amazing and it reminds me of you."

Isabelle had come up short several times in her life, but nothing showed it more than comparing herself to her sister. Juliette had to overcome so much with her skin problems as a teen and had made something good of it.

Was that the trick? Isabelle would have to endure some great tragedy to be blessed as well as her sister?

"I don't know if I could start my own business, Jules. It just seems like a lot of work when all I want to do is design and stage."

"Think about it. I've got a lot of experience myself and would love to get my favorite sister out of the clutches of Darcy Stewart."

Isabelle laughed. "I'm your only sister." After a few moments, she said, "I'll think about it over the weekend and let you know."

"I have a meeting in about five minutes." Juliette paused. "I'm really sorry about Aaron, Isa. I know how much you wanted it to be him."

"Thanks, Jules. I'll let you go." She couldn't mask the resigned tone in her voice and took in a deep breath, feeling more alone than ever.

"You'll figure it out, sis." The line went dead, and Isabelle stared at her phone as if the answer to her problems was going to appear on the screen.

CHAPTER 2

*I*sabelle looked down the street and saw the bus pulling up. The small crowd of people converged, entering one at a time. She shifted her cup of tea to the other hand and pulled out her wallet, tapping it on the scanner. Once the green light gave the okay, she glanced around the packed bus, only finding one spot near the back.

Turning sideways, Isabelle moved around a man chatting loudly with a girl sitting on the bench in front of him. She lengthened her stride, hoping to make it to her seat before the bus started moving. She made it up the first step in the walkway but tripped over the next as the bus lurched forward, sending her sprawling into the empty seat and her tea spraying all over the man sitting next to the window. He looked to be a couple years older than Isabelle, and shame rushed over her at her clumsiness.

His head flicked up, his green eyes seeming to bore through her as his mouth contorted into a frown. He grunted something and wiped his hand over his suit coat. A larger man behind him stood up and handed him a few napkins, as if waiting for a moment like this.

"I am so, so sorry. Can I help?" Isabelle took the seat next to him, picking up one of the napkins and hovering, unsure what she could really do.

He held up a hand, and his deep baritone voice seemed to reverberate through her insides. "Just let me do it, please."

The short snap of his tone caused Isabelle to bite her lower lip, almost drawing blood. She studied him, seeing the muscle near his jaw working as he scrubbed at the spots on what looked like a very expensive suit. Pulling her wallet out of her bag, she handed him one of her few business cards, the ones Darcy had made her buy and pay for by herself.

The man looked up, his eyebrows cinching together. "What's this for?"

"So I can pay for the dry-cleaning bill. It's the least I can do after spilling all over you." She waved her hand at the wet spots and gave a small smile.

He moved to take the business card, and Isabelle was sure his hand could swallow hers whole. After tucking the card into his inside coat pocket, he turned back to the window, clenching and unclenching his fists.

Isabelle watched him, hoping she wasn't the complete cause of his frustration. It wasn't normal in Paris—or even London, for that matter—to strike up a conversation with a complete stranger, but she felt such a curiosity that she couldn't leave it alone. It was something she'd battled throughout her life, butting into people's lives, and she could feel herself giving in to the temptation.

"Are you all right?" she asked, lightly touching his arm.

He turned back to her, his eyes unfocused at first. "I don't travel well."

"In a bus? I could understand that if we were flying or driving a long distance, but I don't worry when I'm on the Tube or the bus." She rested her purse on her lap and twisted the engagement ring on her second-to-last finger. Just another reminder of the pain she'd been reliving the past few days. She glanced over at him again, and his strong jaw moved back and forth as if debating whether or not he wanted to continue the conversation.

"I don't mind flying. If I could fly everywhere I needed to go, even across the city, I'd do it."

"What's got you all worried about driving on streets? Were you in an accident or something?" She raised her eyebrows, wide-eyed. It probably wasn't the right thing to get excited about, but she found an odd fascination in learning about a person's background. It helped her succeed in interior design as well, as she could dig at the things most important for the client. Too bad Darcy didn't always agree with that skill.

Again his jaw flexed, and he finally said, "Yes, a few years ago."

She hadn't seen his entire face, as he kept the right side closest to the window, but his profile drew her in, the strong jaw and green eyes.

He shifted away, sending a small cloud of his cologne toward her. It smelled like the ocean.

Turning to look out the window as she breathed it in, she realized this was her stop. Standing, she held on to the metal bar, waiting for the bus to come to a stop before daring to move forward. Her tea cup was only partially full now, but she didn't want to make the same mistake twice.

"Have a good day. Sorry about your suit." Isabelle gave him a close-lipped smile and turned to walk off the bus and onto the street. The doors closed behind her, and the bus drove on.

She turned to the large department store, heading to the kitchen section. Darcy had requested a certain glass pitcher for an idea she'd had, meaning Isabelle was sent to retrieve it.

Even as she walked, she pictured the man on the bus.

She'd probably never see him again, but what little she'd gathered about him intrigued her.

Shaking her head, she tried to match the picture on her phone to the pitchers on the display. She needed to figure out something for her career so she wouldn't be the errand girl for the rest of her life.

CHAPTER 3

Finally making it to his stop, Roman Hamilton took a deep breath, grateful for one more journey coming to an end without any fanfare. As a thirty-year-old billionaire in London, it was getting harder and harder to do. The tea on his suit was nearly dried now, and as long as that was the only accident that happened while he was trapped in a moving vehicle, he'd be okay.

Waiting for Beau, his bodyguard for public transit, to move in front of him, he stepped down and out of the doors, moving in the direction of his office building.

Beau opened the doors to the towering building that housed Magnolia Property Group, the company Roman's father had started when Roman was a child. It had been designed to accommodate commercial building and real estate sales, but Roman had found there were several under-served housing niches in the city, allowing him to boost the company to its current status over the past few years.

Roman strode past the front desk, nodding to the recep-tionist on the way. Lisa had worked for the company for several years before Roman took over, and she was the perfect face to see once people walked into the building, her warm smile making everyone feel welcome.

There were people at the elevator when he and Beau strode up, and several moved to the side. Roman could see them glancing at him every so often, causing him to grit his teeth. He used to be looked at because he was an attractive guy, but now the scar seemed to dominate everyone's attention.

Entering the elevator, Roman and Beau stepped on together, the rest of the people hanging back. It was for the best anyway. His employees thought of him as demanding and blunt, but it was the only way he'd been able to bring the company back to life after his father's indictment.

Roman pushed his irritation to the back and checked his phone. As he waited for one of his apps to open, he looked over at Beau. "Big weekend plans?" He'd known the man for the past two years, and they'd become close during that time, as close as a bodyguard and his client could become. At least Beau wasn't intimidated by him.

The large man smiled and turned to look at Roman. "My daughter's first birthday. My wife's been planning the party since before Rosie was born. I'm sure it will rival her future wedding."

Roman chuckled, picturing the small Latino woman. She was a firecracker and kept Beau in line, even though he towered over his wife in height and size.

"Good luck," was all Roman could say. Thinking back on all of his birthdays, the parties hadn't really been for him but for his father, Peter Hamilton, to invite investors and other people with money, or toffs they'd call them. There wasn't a family function that didn't factor into his father's work of real estate, which was one of the reasons Roman hadn't wanted to get involved with it in the first place. But now that his father wasn't looking over his shoulder every moment of the day, he realized how much he actually enjoyed the development side of housing.

Making it up to the twelfth floor, they walked out, Beau standing guard next to the elevator and Roman moving down the hall toward his office. Shirley, his assistant, sat at her desk just outside his door, tapping away at the keyboard as if she were trying to break a typing record.

"How was lunch, Shirley? Any messages?" he asked as he turned and opened his office door.

"It was good, thank you, Mr. Hamilton. I have just a couple of calls for you here," she said as she followed him into his office and placed a paper on his desk.

He sat in his swivel chair, trying to get his mind to focus back on work. He kept picturing the woman from the bus, her long dark hair and sea-blue eyes emblazoned in his mind. She'd smelled like a field of spring flowers, and her accent, although faint, intrigued him. It had been a while since he'd run into a French girl. But that wasn't saying much since he tried to go out in public as rarely as possible. At least he'd been able to keep his scar hidden from her so she wouldn't be scared to sit by him, seeing as it had been the only open spot left on the bus.

He leaned forward, picking up the paper Shirley had dropped and read the names. Nodding, he said, "I'll take care of this. Thank you."

"Beth and Anne were trying to contact you earlier. They said your phone kept going to voicemail."

Roman groaned and nodded. "Probably while I was on the bus. Did they say what they needed?"

With a chuckle, Shirley said, "Just that they needed money for going out. They complained that their cards weren't working anymore."

Roman grinned. "That's a good thing. I may be their guardian, but that doesn't mean they get out of earning it.

They're already spoiled as it is." It was always a balancing act when handling his eighteen-year-old twin half-sisters.

Shirley held up her hands. "I'm not arguing that one. They're good girls, but they definitely need some boundaries." She nodded, moving toward the door. "Will there be anything else at the moment, sir?"

Roman closed one eye, trying to think of anything she could help him with. Snapping his fingers, he said, "Make sure we send a present to Beau's daughter, Rosie, for her birthday this weekend."

A wide smile spread over Shirley's face. She loved it when he asked her to send gifts to people. "I'll go start on that right now. Is there an amount you want to spend?"

Roman shrugged. "Make sure she gets anything she needs. I trust you. Just put it on my personal credit card." She'd almost left the room when he said, "Just make sure they don't know who it's from."

Shirley frowned, shaking her head. "I don't know why I can't ever put your name on anything."

"Just go find something for her. I'll take care of the phones while you're gone." Roman smiled, knowing it was the only way to get her to leave.

The thought of attaching his name to any kind of gift sent a shiver down his spine. He enjoyed the thrill of giving the gifts, even if they were over the top, but he didn't like the extra layer of grateful frosting everyone tried to give him when they found out it was from him. He needed people to be real, as he got enough fake sympathy every time someone stared too long at the scar down the side of his face.

He picked up the phone and dialed one of his agents. "Robbie, Shirley told me you called. What do you need?"

"Yeah, I called your phone, but you must not have had service, sir. These apartments over here on the West Side aren't selling. We need to think of something different."

"Well, are you coming to me with problems or solutions?"

The line was silent, and Roman let out a big breath. It was something he'd tried to instill in his employees: when they encountered a problem, they needed to find some way to fix it before calling him.

When Robbie didn't answer after several more seconds, Roman said, "Let me check the plans." His voice was less gruff, and he tried to feel some sympathy for the new hire.

Roman opened his computer and found the image of the row of buildings he'd purchased just a few months ago. They'd been run down, and he'd commissioned to have them gutted and fixed up, new drywall and new paint. He'd thought that splurging on the stainless-steel appliances would have made them attractive for anyone in search of a small-town house, but no one was biting. If they didn't start moving some of the properties, the investment would move into the red in no time.

Robbie finally spoke, surprising Roman with his honesty. "I know I'm new here, sir, but I think these units are too plain. I've seen the benefit of staging, and I think this is one of those times when it might be worth it to hire someone who can make it look homier."

The name of the Magnolia Property Group did a lot of the work for them when it came to selling properties. It had taken some time to build up the brand after his father had been locked up on charges of embezzlement almost five years prior, but under Roman's reign, it had become synonymous with class and high quality.

"Thanks, Robbie. That's just the kind of answer I needed to hear. Do you have any suggestions for a staging company in London?"

"I don't, sir. At my last job, I was taking a couple around to look at properties, and the one that was staged was the one they ended up buying. I can look them up for you, though."

"I'll handle this. Thank you for the suggestion. When I find something, I'll make sure to let you know."

"Thank you, sir. I appreciate it." Robbie's voice sounded more grateful than anyone Roman had talked to all day.

Hanging up, Roman chuckled. Part of him wished people didn't cower in front of him, but it was the only way he knew how to guide and grow his company. At least the people closest to him knew what he was really like.

He reached for a paper in his coat and pulled out the business card the woman on the bus had given him at the same time. Reading it, he saw her name was Isabelle. Below it, he read, *Interior Designer, Stager*.

What were the odds that he needed to look into staging and had met a stager on the bus? Thinking back to their encounter, he smiled. He hadn't met a stranger that forward and talkative since he'd been at university in California. Then again, he didn't think she'd seen his scar yet, and that always changed people's perceptions of him.

Typing in the web address from her card, it took him to the website of a Darcy Stewart. Her picture highlighted the upturned nose, her lips pursed instead of smiling. She wasn't the first person he'd want to work with, as that type of person reminded him of all the snakes his father had worked with over the years. The collection of awards mentioned in her bio did nothing to change his attitude toward her.

Scrolling down a bit, he saw a picture of Isabelle, and for a moment, it was as if she were staring at him in real life. Her hair was in soft curls over her shoulder, and her blue eyes twinkled above the hint of a smile on her face. He'd seen the large ring on her finger, and he knew what that meant.

Shaking his head, he clicked to see some of the projects listed, and an idea formed in his mind.

aking out his cell phone, he punched in the number on the card for a new text message.

Do you have some time to meet me at my office?

He took a breath before pressing send and then realized he hadn't stated who he was.

The guy on the bus.

He set his phone down and looked over the note Shirley had left him, trying to order them in importance. He picked up his desk phone and had dialed a few numbers, when his phone vibrated on his desk. Swiping, he saw it was Isabelle.

You can just send me the bill. Or just tell me when to pay it.

Roman tapped his finger against his mouth, trying to figure out what to say.

I'd like to talk about staging some properties. I saw that's what you do on your card.

Only a few seconds ticked by before she replied.

Oh, I can do that. Send me your address.

After sending it to her, he watched the phone, waiting for her answer to pop up. Again, it was only a few seconds, and he wondered how fast she could type at that rate.

I'm only a few blocks away. I'll be there in about fifteen minutes.

For some reason, her answer sent a thrill through his upper body, and he moved to check his appearance in the mirror. He rubbed his thumb along the scar that stretched from his right eyebrow down to just below his right ear. It was still bright pink, even five years since the accident, but at least the pain was subsiding.

Looking around the room, he straightened up a few papers and then made a call down to Lisa so she would know to let Isabelle in.

What was he so panicked for? There was no way a beautiful girl like that would like him in that way. He used to think he'd hit the jackpot when it came to looks, but now all he saw was the scar, and so did everyone else. Having a conversation with someone off the street was almost impossible as he'd watch them stare at the slice the plastic surgeon had worked hours to stitch together.

He hadn't even looked at girls since, as his work took priority over everything, even a casual relationship. Being the guardian to his twin half-sisters didn't make things easier. When he wasn't working, he was keeping up with them, making sure they had some discipline in their life.

He thought about a few of the women he'd taken to events since his accident. None of them wanted to be second to anything, especially emergency work calls that came late at night. He'd learned to read people well throughout his time in real estate, and though many women wanted to be with him because of his fortune, how long would that last before they were bored and left him?

Time passed faster than he'd expected, and he heard a sound coming from his phone. "Isabelle Rousseau is on her way up, Mr. Hamilton."

Pressing a button, he leaned in and said, "Thanks, Lisa."

Standing up, he buttoned the top two buttons on his coat and walked out by the elevators. Beau looked in his direction and straightened, as if he could be causing trouble standing by the elevator.

"The woman from the bus is on her way up. Will you show her to my office when she arrives?"

Beau's eyebrow raised, as did the corners of his mouth. "Certainly."

The grin made Roman defensive. "Don't give me that look. She's just coming for some business. She's a stager, and I think she's engaged."

"I didn't say anything, sir." Beau's smile grew wider, as if he knew something that could never happen in the real world.

Without giving a second response, Roman spun on his heel and walked back to his office. Settling in behind the desk again, he pulled up the information for the properties and printed several pictures and sets of information. Forty units. All empty and waiting for tenants.

As he gazed at the pictures, he was surprised at the change that just a bit of money and some skilled craftsmen could create in what was once a run-down part of London.

A knock on the door caused his head to shoot up, and Isabelle leaned in.

"This is your office, huh?" she said, glancing around. Her eyes locked onto the view outside, a landscape of the city. It had been the reason he wanted this office and not a corner view on the other side of the floor. The corner office showed a section of the business district, the beauty not inspiring in the least.

He stood and walked to her, stopping a few feet away. Instead of looking out the window at what she was seeing, he studied her face, trying to tamp down the wild emotions taking over his chest.

"Yep. This is where I work."

She broke her gaze away from the window and looked at him, her eyes moving over his scar. A mixture of emotions passed over her face, from terror to sadness to sympathy. Nothing he hadn't seen before. She moved a large bag from one hand to the other.

"What happened? Was this from your accident?" She took a step forward, and Roman was surprised when her finger caressed the length of the scar, her touch like a lightning rod. He hadn't been touched by anyone like that in donkey's years.

It took a moment for his mind to clear enough to say anything coherent, and he turned away, trying to hide the deformity from her inspection. "Yes." That was the most he could muster at the moment.

He glanced up out of the corner of his eye to watch her face as she realized what she was doing, how close she was to him, and took a step back. As a red hue highlighted her cheekbones, she asked, "What was it you wanted to see me about?"

Her eyes drew him in, those dark blue pools next to long dark lashes…he needed to focus on the task at hand. He didn't need a broken heart while he had so many deals to work on in the coming weeks. A girl like Isabelle was a walking heartbreaker. Why he was even worried, he couldn't figure out, since the large rock sat firmly on her left hand.

"I have several properties that aren't selling like our company is used to. I wanted to get your feedback on staging and see if it's something we need to do company-wide." He waved her past him. "Please, have a seat over there, Ms. Rousseau."

She set her package by the door and moved past him, her light floral scent hitting him again.

Roman took a seat next to her, pushing the papers toward

her. "Our company bought a tract of houses a few months ago and remodeled them. They are perfect for single people or even small families. We are used to having our properties sell within the first few days, but we haven't sold any here."

Isabelle took the papers, her eyes squinting every once in a while as she looked at the pictures. It was several minutes before she looked up at him.

"I think these definitely need staging. With all of the white walls and empty space, it doesn't draw me in, doesn't make me want to live there. But with a light color on the wall and several furnishings, I think you'll have several offers after an open house." She handed the papers back to him and stood, pulling her bag over her shoulder.

Roman stood. He was used to being the one who said when meetings were over, and he didn't want her to go just yet.

He nodded, giving her a half-smile. "This might seem like a lame question, but do you think it's worth it? Do the sellers recoup the costs they spend on you when they finally sell?"

She turned toward him, her eyes searching his face with suspicion before nodding. "I've been laughed at for my profession by many people who sell homes, as many people think of it as a scam, but some people just need the vision of what their life can look like in that space. Some of them even pay for us to leave the furniture and accessories there."

"Do you give bids?"

"Uh, well, the woman I work for would send it to you, but they would be numbers I figured."

"What if I wanted to just hire you? Will you do it for me? Stage one of the units?"

Isabelle shifted her feet. "Well, um, I guess. But I would probably lose my job over it. I'm sure Darcy would love to get a contract from Magnolia." She said the words with distaste, as if disappointed about something.

"Do you get commissions from bringing in clients?" As a real estate agent, he was used to compensating people for referrals, knowing that was one of the best ways to keep his business running.

Isabelle shook her head. "I'm just a glorified secretary. I don't get any extras for anything."

Roman raised his hand to his chin, cupping it between his thumb and pointer finger. "What if I hire you to do it as a side job?"

Her mouth parted, and her eyebrows went up, as if considering his proposal. She finally shook her head. "I can't. Darcy would kill me if I did something without her approval."

"Do you always do what she wants you to?" Frustration surged in him, and he couldn't think of another way to get what he wanted.

"Well, yes, no. I don't know. She's just one of those people you don't cross. If I ever want a chance to do interior design and staging for real, having her recommendation would open doors I couldn't open on my own."

Roman stuffed his hands into his pockets. "I won't tell her if you don't. Just stage one of these units for me, enough that we can get pictures taken for the listings and have an open house. If it works out well, we can figure out where to go from there. If it's a botch job, then you still have your job with Ms. Stewart."

He watched as her chin tilted up and her hand went to her hip. "I promise you, sir, this will not be a botch job. What's your name anyway?"

"Roman Hamilton."

Her brow furrowed. "Sounds familiar. You're probably one of the higher-ups in this company, right?" When the words left her mouth, she paused, her eyes wide open in terror.

Roman chuckled. "I'm just one of many here at Magnolia. But if I don't come up with something to get these units sold, the company is going to lose a lot of money, and then the big boss won't be chuffed about it."

As much as he tried to keep his identity and billionaire status a secret, more and more people knew who he was. If they weren't staring at his scar, they were doing their best to suck up to him for money or connections. Whoever said having money would make life easier must not have had money at all. Knowing she didn't realize who he was put him even more at ease.

"Nice to meet you, Mr. Hamilton. Do you mind if I think it over tonight?" she asked.

Nodding, Roman grabbed a business card from his desk and handed it to her. "Of course, and please call me Roman. Just let me know your decision in the morning. If you don't do it, I'll have to look for another company."

Isabelle cocked her head to the side, her eyebrows cinching together. "Why don't you just go through my boss?"

Roman let out a little laugh. "I already looked up the company. She doesn't look like someone I'm willing to deal with, even for a conversation."

To his surprise, a wide grin took over her face, and it made her eyes twinkle. She opened her mouth as if to say something in response but closed it, nodding.

"Okay, I'll let you know tomorrow what I decide." She walked back to the wall and picked up her large bag. "If you don't mind, I have to get this back to the office, or Darcy will be furious." She nodded goodbye and slipped out the door.

Roman kept rooted to the spot, willing himself not to watch her leave. There was something about her that he couldn't quite get. She was so outgoing that she could have almost any job she wanted. But he knew things in interior design could be cutthroat, just from what others had told him during his time in real estate. It was one of the reasons he'd steered clear of them until now.

He stared out the window, hoping she'd accept his offer. Seeing the look in her eyes as she'd noticed the thick scar on his face should have been like every other person who'd stare at him for several minutes at a time, but it wasn't. She'd even touched the scar without flinching. For some reason, he hoped she'd look past it and see him for who he really was: just a man, trying to figure out what his role in life was ever since his deformity had occurred.

If her boss was anything like how he pictured her, and if Isabelle was as attuned to details as she seemed to be, she'd accept his offer. He just hoped it would happen sooner rather than later. They needed the units to move and now.

CHAPTER 5

Isabelle wasn't sure why Roman had given her a business card since she already had his number from his text earlier. She held onto it as she boarded the bus, situating her things around her as she took a forward-facing seat near the middle.

Her insides still buzzed from their conversation, tainted partly by the fact that she'd been so forward. She was usually more aware of her surroundings and social cues, but for some reason, she'd felt drawn to Roman. His scar looked as though it had happened within the past few years, the bright pink slice down his face standing out.

She could still feel the smooth scar as she'd lightly touched it, only noticing how close she'd been once he flinched. The tingles his skin had sent through her fingers had blocked her warning cues to keep her distance. For some reason, the touch felt a lot more intense than just touching a stranger's face. Compassion for what he must have gone through flooded her, driving her to want to earn his trust enough that he'd tell her his story.

On the bus, he'd been attractive but terse. In his office,

he'd looked vulnerable, as if turning himself inside out and showing her everything. With the scar noticeable, it drew her eyes to his emerald green ones and then to his strong jaw. How someone could look that good and have a scar like that, she wasn't sure. But she'd have to be careful she didn't get too attached.

She looked down at the black card in her hand, the lettering white and embossed. Roman Hamilton. Magnolia Property Group. Chief Executive Officer.

He was the head boss? Why had she thought he was just one of the real estate agents? Taking in a deep breath, she wondered what to do.

It was a tempting thought, to have a client where she didn't have Darcy breathing down her neck, but she wasn't sure she was ready for the unknown of unemployment.

Twenty minutes later, she walked into the main office for Stewart Design, and as if sensing it was Isabelle, Darcy's voice echoed throughout the office.

"Isabelle! Get into my office right now!"

Darcy Stewart was the top interior designer and stager in all of London. A social climber, she worked to further her connections, hoping to spread her name and influence around all of Europe. She was a tall, slender woman, and rumor had it she'd been one of the top models in her day. How she had landed in the design business, Isabelle wasn't quite sure and never had the guts to ask.

"Yes, Miss Darcy?" Isabelle peeked around the corner into the office, trying to look more casual than scared.

"Where are we on the Ashford project? I just got off the phone with Brandon Ashford, and he said they've been waiting for the light fixtures for the last two weeks. Did you even order them?" Darcy's forehead creased, her lips pursing as if she tasted something bitter.

Looking down first at her phone and then at a small notebook she carried with her, Isabelle flipped through the pages, holding her breath in the hopes that she had written something down. Finding a page with several doodle marks and prices with *light fixtures* written next to it helped her to release the air bit by bit.

"They were on backorder as of the twenty-fifth. I'll call again and get a rush order placed on them." Isabelle tried to smile, but the look she got from Darcy caused her to retreat.

"I just promised him they would be in by the end of the week. Make sure it happens, or it will be your fault that the project isn't completed on time."

"I understand." Isabelle threw back her shoulders, hoping her boss couldn't see the nervous energy causing her limbs to shake. She usually thought of herself as a strong person, but for some reason, Darcy put the fear of everything into her.

Walking over, Isabelle leaned in and waited.

Darcy looked up at her finally. "Did you find the pitcher?"

She lifted the bag and set it on Darcy's desk before leaning back against the doorframe as her boss opened the package.

"Is this the best they had? I thought I sent you the picture of the one I wanted."

Trying to calm her rising irritation, Isabelle said, "This was the same as the picture. It even has the same serial number you sent me."

Darcy rolled her eyes. "I don't like it. Take it back."

"Okay." It was all Isabelle could say without getting snarky. She knew Darcy wouldn't respond well to her snark.

"I also need you to pick up several boxes from a store downtown."

Looking at the large silver clock on the wall, Isabelle said, "Tonight? Will they still be open at this hour?"

Darcy gave her a fake smile, and her sugary tone told Isabelle she wasn't pleased. "Some stores work later than five on a Friday. I need to get all the supplies together because we need to get this house staged on Wednesday."

"Can I take one of the vans? I won't be able to carry all the boxes with me on the bus."

With a sigh, Darcy said, "I guess. Just make sure it comes back dent-free, or it will come out of your pay."

Isabelle moved out of her boss' office before she'd finished speaking, not wanting to hear the "don't break anything" speech one more time. Carrying the bag with the pitcher, she grabbed a set of keys from the board before she left for the parking lot in back, hoping she could get this all done before it was too late.

As she started the van, she adjusted the radio station to play some of her favorite tunes and dialed the company for the light fixtures. All hope of getting the rush order in quickly went out the window as the horrendous elevator music played, and from past experience, she knew she'd be on the line for at least thirty minutes. It would be better to call Monday morning and see what they could do.

She put the van into reverse and merged with the London traffic, watching all the happy people going home on a Friday afternoon.

It took much longer than she wanted but she finally arrived at the store, parking in a stall. As the frustration surged from thinking about all that had happened today, she clicked her phone on and opened the message from Roman earlier.

I'll do it. I can start tomorrow if you want.

It didn't take long for his answer to come through.

Awesome! Thank you. Let me know what you need.

That caused her to pause. What would she need for this job? She wished she'd kept the pictures he'd shown her at his office. She'd need to start coming up with ideas as soon as possible because once work began at the house Darcy was staging next week, she wouldn't have a moment free.

When can I see the property?

Tomorrow morning if you're available.

Perfect. Will you email me the details and those pictures? I want to get some preliminary ideas going when I get home tonight.

Will do. Thanks again.

Could she pull off staging a town house in four days?

She wasn't sure, but she knew she needed to do something before Darcy sucked all the creativity out of her.

"Roman, what are you doing here? I thought I booked the 6:53 pm to Paris." Shirley's voice floated in that evening, causing Roman to duck his chin a little bit. She didn't like it when she went to the trouble of making arrangements for him and then he didn't need them.

"Change of plans. The guy I was meeting couldn't make it at that time, some family emergency. I pushed the flight back to Sunday night. I'm meeting a stager tomorrow morning and will need to get a few other things ready before I head out. It's a big acquisition, and I don't feel as prepared as I want to."

"A stager, huh? That's something I never thought I'd hear you say." She gave him a wry smile, causing Roman to chuckle.

Nodding, he said, "Yeah, well, if it will help sell some things, I just might have to eat my words. Did you find something for Rosie?"

A wide grin spread across her face. "Yes. Several toys and one of those rocking horses. I'm sure she'll love it."

"I think you just like spending my money." Roman turned

his head to the side, looking at her out of the corner of his eye.

"Well, you never do, so I may as well. It's five o'clock now, which means I'm off the clock. I've sent the presents to Beau's house so you won't be identified. Have a good flight, and let me know how it goes." His secretary smiled and waved, the silver streaks in her hair shining under the darkening light.

With his email inbox all sorted, replies sent, and appointments made, Roman leaned back, glancing out the window. He should really get the numbers all put together for the meeting he'd have once he got to Paris, but he was ready to go home. He'd been working late almost every night, and if he was going to be gone for the first part of next week, he'd need to get home and see how his half-sisters were faring.

His stepmother had decided she didn't want to be married anymore about a year before Roman's father, Peter, had been indicted. She didn't want to take the eleven-year-old twins with her either, leaving them for his father to take care of. When Peter had gone to prison when they were twelve, the burden had fallen on Roman to take care of the two girls. It had been quite the adjustment to go from a twenty-five-year-old bachelor to the parent of tweens, but they'd somehow survived it.

He'd had to learn how to act as a father-figure, but their relationship had gone well over the past few years. They were eighteen now and about to head off to university.

He dialed Beth on his way out to the car, hoping she would answer. After two rings, she picked up.

"Beth, are you and Anne at home?" He listened in, trying to hear any background noise.

"Yeah, but we're getting ready to go out. Where are you?"

"I'm on my way home. Don't leave until I get there, will you?" He heard a loud sigh come from the other line and smiled. That was like making a kid wait for sticky toffee pudding.

"Fine. But you'd better hurry. We're meeting the girls at seven."

He took a detour, getting past some of the heavy traffic and making it back to the house on Cowley Street at a quarter to seven. Walking in, he switched on a few lights and then took the stairs, looking for the girls. He knocked on their door, waiting for their response rather than barging in.

"Come in."

He walked in and almost choked from the thickness of the perfumes in the air. "Did you bathe in this stuff?" He cough-laughed as he waved a hand at the air in front of his face.

Anne gave him a fake frown. "No, we were just trying to see which would work. Is there one you like the smell of?"

"I can't distinguish them from each other. It just smells like flowers with other perfumes." He almost gagged, and Beth walked out of the closet in a dress that rose up too far on her legs. "Nope. You're not wearing that out unless you put on some of those stretchy trousers or jeans underneath it."

Beth scrunched her nose and narrowed her eyes at him. "You're not my father."

Walking up to her, Roman put both his hands on her shoulders. "Beth, we've talked about this. I'm your big brother, and I just want what's best for you. Besides, I can cut off your allowance. Will you just try something else on first?"

She frowned at him for several more seconds until her shoulders slumped forward. "Fine. I probably wouldn't be comfortable in it all night anyway."

Beth disappeared back into the large walk-in closet the girls shared, and Anne twirled before him. "What do you think?"

She wore a bright pink sleeveless shirt and a mid-thigh jean skirt. At least everything was covered. "You look good, Anne. You're not meeting up with any boys, right?"

Anne gave him a coy expression. "Not that we know of yet."

"You know the rules, Anne. Just be careful, and I want both of you back here by one in the morning."

Clasping her hands in front of her face, Anne knelt on the ground before him. "Can we stay out longer tonight? Please, Roman? None of the others have a curfew."

He looked at her, and her pleading expression made him want to laugh. Sometimes he was surprised they'd survived this long under his care. "Okay, one thirty, but you better not be late. I'll set an alarm to make sure you're here."

Anne stood, not as excited as he thought she should be. He knew how it was, and when he was their age, he'd been able to stay out as long as he wanted. But he also believed that girls were a different breed, and he worried they'd be attacked or hurt somewhere and he wouldn't know where to look for them.

Beth came out of the closet. "Thirty minutes is all you're giving us? We need to find you a girl. Maybe then you'll ease up."

Leave it to Beth to be the one to test him. Anne was the sweet, innocent one for the most part, while her sister, born two minutes earlier, seemed to enjoy confrontation and creating friction.

"Come back by one thirty, and we'll see. You'll be heading to university in a few weeks anyway, and I won't be there to make sure you stay out of trouble, whereas here, I am. I have a lot to worry about with work, and I just want to make sure you are both safe."

He watched as Beth's eyes worked around the room, and then she nodded, satisfied with that answer. She grinned.

"Then you'll really need a girl. This place is so quiet as it is. Anne, who do we know that we could set Roman up with?"

Shaking his head, he stood, making his way to the door. "Don't try to set me up with anyone. Just, no." He paused a moment, enjoying the tight glare Beth shot him. "I'll be fine. You two have a good night, and make sure to check in when you get home."

Walking out of their room, he made his way downstairs, needing to wind down. After changing into some gym shorts and a t-shirt, he sat back in his recliner and flipped through the channels.

Beth's words kept worming their way into his thoughts, and his mind kept calling up an image of Isabelle. She was beautiful but probably not interested in someone like him. Not to mention that she appeared to be engaged.

He just needed to focus on getting the units sold and winning over the negotiation for the property just outside of Paris he'd been eyeing for some time. Goals he could handle. A woman's heart, not so much.

CHAPTER 7

*I*sabelle leaned against the wall of the building, nervously drumming her hands on her legs as she waited next to the row of brick town houses. She'd changed her mind about working with Roman at least a dozen times throughout the night and even that morning before she'd left her small apartment. The idea of staging a home sans Darcy thrilled her, but it also brought to mind how much she depended on it for her daily survival. Her flatmate wasn't the easiest person to live with, and she wouldn't be granted an extension on helping with the rent payment should she lose her job.

Stepping away from the building, she looked up to the third story and then down the road to the end of the street. There were at least fifteen doors along the front, with a large dumpster at the other side of the road. Taking in a deep breath, she hoped Darcy would never find out about this. Who was she kidding? Darcy had eyes everywhere it seemed. She'd find out about this side scheme for sure.

A stab of panic hit her in the chest, convincing her to bail on Roman. She willed her legs to walk calmly along, even though they wanted to take off at a sprint to get out of there before she was caught by someone connected to her employer.

She wished she could walk in the opposite direction, but the bus stop would be closer to the other end, meaning she'd need to walk past the entirety of the building. After making it to the end, she turned to look back, curious as to whether her mind had made the whole thing up or if someone was following her. When she saw nothing down the lane, she chuckled, realizing how paranoid she'd become that morning.

Taking a few steps forward while still looking behind her, she bumped into something hard. She went flying backward until someone caught her arm, stopping her progress toward the ground. Looking up, she squinted, trying to see who it was with the sun shrouding his head.

"Did you forget something?" Roman pulled her up, holding on to her long enough for her to gain her balance, and then let go. She hadn't realized it until he was no longer touching her, but she felt a measure of heat where his fingers had been. Roman was an attractive man, but he was the head of a large real estate firm, not someone who'd be interested in an artist's daughter.

"Uh, no. I...I was trying to decide if I was in the right spot." She hoped the small lie was convincing enough because looking at his straight white teeth and bright green eyes made her stomach flip.

Roman took a step in the direction she'd just come, waiting for her to do the same. "Good. I'm sorry I'm a little late. My sisters came home later than curfew, and we had a lengthy discussion."

"Sisters?" Isabelle was curious about his role as discipliner.

Nodding, he said, "Twin sisters. They're half-sisters,

really. My mother died when I was a child, and theirs decided a few years ago that she didn't want to be a mother anymore. I've been taking care of them since my father… well, since my father went away."

He looked at her as though trying to decide something, maybe wondering if he should've told her these details about his life.

"So, you're their guardian. That seems like a lot to go along with heading up a large company. How old are they?"

The corners of his mouth turned up. "Eighteen. They head to Uni in a month. I don't know who's more excited, me or them."

Isabelle laughed, and she could only imagine what an early morning discussion had been like in Roman's home. "I'm sure you'll miss them. Life has a way of doing that, making us even more grateful for the people in our lives after they're gone. Or ungrateful. I guess it depends on the person."

They walked down a few doors, when Roman turned and pulled a set of keys from his pocket. While he unlocked the door, he asked, "Is there someone you're glad isn't a part of your life anymore?" His intense eyes turned to study her, and Isabelle reached out to steady herself on the brick wall.

"Let's just say I'm still trying to figure that out." She wasn't in the mood to talk about Aaron more than that, as the feelings were still too raw.

The door opened, and he waved her in before him.

As she entered, Isabelle tried to keep her mind focused, even as the smell of a fresh breeze carrying his cologne wrapped around her. Taking in the room, she was surprised.

Isabelle had been through a lot of homes and apartments in the few years she'd been staging, but this had to be the most plain she'd ever seen a dwelling. Every wall was white, while the carpet smelled new but was an ugly beige. She moved into the kitchen and was surprised to see granite countertops and basic stainless steel appliances.

Turning to Roman, she asked, "Do you rent these out? Or are you hoping to sell them?"

"I'd prefer to sell them as a town house. I have—our company has enough rental properties as it is, and this was more of an investment than anything."

"When was this renovated?"

"About three months ago."

Isabelle nodded, biting one side of her cheek as she thought.

She wandered into the bedrooms, finding the same stark-white walls and ugly carpet. The one good thing was the large master closet and somewhat-decent bathroom.

"Did you have a designer on the job at all?"

Roman grimaced. "No, we used a new contractor who claimed he had a designer, but from the looks of it, he didn't do much more than the absolute minimum. That's something I need to address." He pulled out his phone and typed for a few seconds before putting it away.

"What would happen if you lost that?" Isabelle smiled as she gestured to his coat pocket.

Roman's eyes went wide, and he smiled, his head turned a bit to the side. "I'd probably run around like a chicken with my head cut off. It's got my life in there. Probably not the best thing, but business never sleeps it seems." He adjusted his stance and placed one hand over the right side of his face, his other arm propping up his elbow. It looked like a defense mechanism more than anything, as his eyes kept straying from hers to the countertop and back. It saddened her to think he worried about hiding his scar. "From all the questions about the place, I take it you have some ideas?"

She saw the hopeful look on his face and smiled. "Yes, I have quite a few ideas that should get them ready to sell within a week of finishing. White is the worst color for an entire apartment. This solid-color carpet shows stains and looks cheap. The granite looks good, but an upgrade on the fridge might be a good option. Not essential like the other things, but always a good selling point."

Roman pulled out his phone again and typed something. "Sorry, they're installing the carpet in some of the end units later today. I'm just going to stop that and let you pick out a good carpet, reasonable but something that would attract people to buy." His face was focused as he placed the phone near his ear and waited.

Isabelle turned away, surprised that he was making changes like that just from her suggestions. There weren't many times in her life when people had done that, and a feeling of pride swelled within her.

"So, how much do you think it would cost?" Roman's voice brought her around.

Isabelle sighed. "This is a rough estimate as I'd need to check a few things, like the price per square foot of the carpet I'm thinking of, and with the dimensions of the rooms, I could calculate paint. Probably five to ten thousand."

"For this unit? That includes new carpet, paint, a new fridge, finishes, and labor?" Roman's voice didn't sound like it was accusing her of anything, even though she thought he should.

"Yes," Isabelle said with a slight hesitation. Was that too much? With forty units, just a few thousand pounds added up quickly.

She expected him to freak out, but he nodded his head, rubbing his chin as he looked at something near her feet. "What will it cost for the staging furniture?"

Isabelle glanced around and made a mental map of the floor plan, trying to think of different elements that would work in the space. "A high estimate would be two thousand pounds."

"And then your fee." Roman's eyes were averted making her wonder if he was asking for what she charged or if he meant it as a hypothetical question. "Okay, let's do it. We stayed under budget on our renovations with a couple of jammy breaks, so these little upgrades won't hurt. We'll start with this town house, and then we can go from there. We'll change out the carpets in all of the units. Maybe using three different colors of carpet?"

"Yeah, I can keep that in mind. So, this one unit, like a trial run?"

Roman nodded. "Honestly, using any kind of interior designer or stager is new ground for me. I think we'll evaluate how it goes after this one is finished and go from there."

"It might be a good idea to paint some of the other properties and then have this as your open house unit until you've sold several. It would save you money on the staging." What was she doing? That would mean she wouldn't make as much money and was probably a sign that she shouldn't run her own business.

He looked like he was thinking something over before he said, "Good idea. What do you need from me to get started?"

Isabelle bit her bottom lip, not sure she should actually say what she needed. She thought about her bank account at the moment, and she'd be lucky to make it through another month with the dismal amount held there. There was no way it would cover what she'd need for this project.

"Don't take this the wrong way, but do you have accounts with different companies? Or how do you want me to work payment of the items and labor?" She braced herself, familiar with Darcy's overreaction to nearly everything Isabelle asked for.

Roman chuckled, the sound deep and attractive. He

pulled out his wallet from his back pocket and pulled out a card, handing it over to her. "I'll have my secretary, Shirley, order one for you. But until it comes in, just use that one."

Taking the card from him, their fingers touched at the tips, sending energy sparking through her arm to the shoulder. Isabelle looked at the card to find a landscape on it, a beautiful sunset with the pinks and purples and reds stretching across the sky. She wondered if it was a standard card face or if he'd chosen the picture.

Turning back to him, she asked, "I meant to ask earlier. Did you get your suit to the cleaner? I still owe you for that."

Roman waved a hand at her. "If you do as amazing with this project as I think you will, that will more than make up for it." He smiled, revealing a dimple near the long scar on the side of his face. She could feel his eyes on her as she studied his features, and she glanced away, tucking a stray piece of hair behind her ear.

"Thank you. Well, I guess I'd better get to work on it, then." Isabelle smiled at him, trying to decide if she should just say goodbye and walk out of the town house. Having a company card in her wallet without the long list of restrictions Darcy usually included when she left the office felt somewhat freeing. She wouldn't abuse it, but it was nice that someone could trust her so easily.

"Okay. Let me know if you need anything. Do you think you could have it done by next weekend?" He looked at her hopefully, and Isabelle could only laugh.

"Let me see what I can do. If all the pieces I need can get here that soon, we could probably have an open house by next Saturday."

Roman nodded. "I'm heading out of town tomorrow night for a meeting, but you can call me for any problems or questions you have."

They walked out the door, and Isabelle turned toward the

bus stop. "Can I drop you off somewhere? I've got a car just around the corner."

Raising an eyebrow, she said, "I thought you don't like driving in cars."

"I make an exception when my driver is available."

Roman led the way to the dark black limo around the corner and opened the door, waiting to enter until she got in. She wasn't sure what kind of world she'd stumbled into when she'd spilled her tea on him yesterday, but it was unlike anything she'd ever experienced.

CHAPTER 8

"Good morning, Shirley. Will you send me the number for the contractor we used on the Hillside Towers renovation?" Roman sat back in the chair in his Paris hotel room, going through emails and trying to get everything taken care of before he spent the afternoon in meetings.

"Sure, what's wrong?" Shirley asked.

Roman groaned. "I should've gone over there a few months ago to check on things, but I dropped the ball. The contractor cut corners and pocketed the extra money. I just want to have a friendly chat with him."

"And by friendly chat, you mean—"

"I mean I'll let him know his chance to work with us again has passed while serving him with papers to get the money back. I'll make sure to say please and thank you."

Shirley's deep laugh caused Roman to chuckle. "Will do. I sent the paperwork for the building to Isabelle Rousseau on Saturday, as asked. How did it go, walking through the place with her?"

"Good, I guess. She seemed to know her stuff. Asked a lot

of good questions and made me recall the carpet we'd put into several of the units already. I'm thinking it will be good to get her insight on some things, but we'll see."

"And? Is she a nice girl?"

"I know what you're asking, Shirley. She's a nice girl, very pretty. But I think she's engaged, and I don't have time for dating."

"I run your calendar. Maybe I should block out time for dates." Her words trailed higher at the end, the tone teasing.

"Yeah, but then you wouldn't have anything to do. Just send me his number, and I'll get things taken care of."

Roman hung up the phone and made his way down to the lobby of the hotel. Once outside, he moved in the direction of his favorite patisserie, one he visited each time he was in the city. He came to Paris often to see his frat brother Tristan. It was usually the only time Roman relaxed, unless Tristan had some new marketing scheme to implement for the Magnolia Property Group. Tristan was good at his job, and Roman could always see the bump in sales after something new Tristan had put into place.

Roman found a table in the corner and took a sip of his coffee, trying to ease his mind before the meetings later that afternoon. The bell above the door rang, and in walked a tall dark-haired man.

Roman's face split into a grin. He let Tristan order and then waved to him. Tristan gave him a nod and moved in his direction.

"You're late. No girlfriend today, huh?" Roman joked. He'd heard all about how things had gone with Tristan and a girl named Juliette. First Jackson—another frat brother—and now Tristan.

Something in Roman's chest squeezed, and he wondered what had caused it. He just hoped it wasn't expected for him to be the next to propose to a girl. He didn't even know if he could get a girl to date him anymore.

"She works too, man. How was the flight?" Tristan said, taking a bite of his tartelette.

"It was good. Always better than driving."

"I agree with that, and I'm not even afraid of cars." The two of them chuckled, and Roman was grateful for their friendship and that his friends understood the terror that filled him every time he got into a car now.

"If it weren't for Sam and his driving skills, I probably wouldn't ever get into a car again. And it's nice to have a driver who is also my pilot as well."

"I'm surprised he doesn't also work as your bodyguard."

Roman chuckled. "Beau does a great job and I really only need him for things in the city when I use public transport."

"Maybe we just need to find you a girl. A lot of fears can be solved with a girl in your life." Tristan grinned, and Roman slugged him in the shoulder.

Shaking his head, Roman said, "How is dating someone going to help me get over my fear of cars?"

Tristan shrugged. "I don't know. But you'd be surprised what a girlfriend can do for you."

Picking up his cup, Roman took a long draw before setting it back down again. "It was hard enough to find a genuine girl before the accident because all they wanted was my money. Now it's hard to get anyone to come near me because of my scar."

"Or because you're ornery around them, almost like a beast."

Roman frowned, not sure he wanted to go into this any further. Isabelle's face kept popping up in his mind, and he smiled. "I did meet a girl the other day who isn't scared of me."

"How did you meet her?" Tristan lifted a napkin to the corner of his mouth, wiping away some cream.

"The bus. She tripped and spilled her tea all over me."

Tristan gave him an incredulous look. "You were on the bus?"

"Sam's wife has been sick, and I still have nightmares from the one time Beau drove me just a few streets from the office. So I improvised."

Tristan's deep laugh grew in volume, and before long, he was laughing so hard it turned into a cough. "I'm sure that was interesting. I can see you doing everything you could to hide your scar. But at least riding the bus is something the old Roman would have done. Maybe you're coming back to your old self after all."

Roman took a bite from the croissant in front of him. "Anyway, I hired the girl to stage one of the units in some town houses that haven't been selling."

"You hired a girl after she spilled tea all over you? Have you asked her out yet?" Tristan hadn't wiped the grin off his face since Roman started the story, and it was getting old. Roman was tempted to wallop him.

He shook his head. "She has a ring on, so I'm pretty sure she's engaged."

"Pretty sure means you're just assuming. You should ask her. If she's not, you've already eliminated one of your blockades to a relationship with her. You'd just have to figure out if she'd be with you for your money or not."

Taking in a breath, Roman's mind flashed back to when he'd said his name, sure she'd heard about his net worth. "I don't think she knows who I am, which I'm fine with."

"That could backfire, though. What if she's uncomfortable with people who have a lot of money?"

Leaning forward, Roman studied Tristan's face. "Is there such a person?"

"Well, relationships aren't all a piece of tartelette, but Juliette figured out how to get past the money."

Roman took another sip from his cup, savoring the warm liquid before swallowing. He had a sudden urge to know if Isabelle was really engaged. But did he really want a relationship?

Looking at Tristan's contented face, he knew Juliette had helped him a lot in the short time they'd been dating. But a happily ever after wasn't something that could happen to Roman. He'd been let down too many times to count throughout his life, and a pretty girl agreeing to put together a town house for him wasn't a guarantee of anything but an increase in sales.

CHAPTER 9

*L*ater that afternoon, Roman found himself sitting in front of Silvain Guilbert, owner of a large tract of land and industrial and residential buildings on the outskirts of Paris. Roman had been looking into the land since he'd taken his father's place in the business, knowing it would be a great investment and, with a little work, would be perfect for his company.

"Now that we've eaten, young man, let's get to why you're here." Silvain pushed his plate a few inches, allowing him to place a folder in front of him.

Roman pulled out a packet of papers from his briefcase, feeling satisfied with the negotiations he'd detailed within it. It had been his best work to date, and he wanted to see the older man's surprise at such a thorough plan for his land.

After handing the papers to Silvain, he leaned back, slicing through a small piece of cake and savoring the richness of it. "I've taken several numbers from what I could find and put together what I think your property is currently worth, based upon others close by."

Roman kept quiet as the man flipped through a few of the

papers, stopping every now and again. After several minutes, the white-haired man looked up with a blank expression and stared at Roman. Trying not to squirm, Roman stared back, hoping to pass whatever test this was turning into.

"Why do you want my land, Mr. Hamilton?" Silvain cut into his own pastry, silence surrounding them as Roman's mind spun. What was the answer to that?

Blowing out a breath, he said, "It's a great piece of property, sir. Close to the city but still out enough to not worry about the traffic. I've built up Magnolia Property Group by finding the buildings that would benefit from sprucing, and I feel like yours fall into that category."

Holding up the pile of papers, Silvain said, "Looks like you've done a thorough job of this."

Roman smiled. "Thank you, sir."

"The offer sounds intriguing. But I have my reservations. You might not have known from doing your research, but I was a victim of one of your father's schemes back in the day. I have seen that, overall, you're an upstanding young lad, but with something of this scale, how do I know you won't go tearing everything down and creating some kind of resort?"

Swallowing with more force than he wanted, Roman tugged at his collar, feeling like he'd been baking in the sun. He hadn't felt like that in a few years, since he'd been able to separate his reputation from his father's.

After bowing his head for a moment, Roman looked back up, meeting Silvain's eyes. "I am deeply sorry, sir. You are correct in that I didn't know you'd known my father. I have been slowly paying back everything he took. What amount did he owe you? I will get it repaid." The new information blindsided Roman. Would he ever be able to say he was finally done cleaning up his father's mess?

The man's lips twitched and then turned upward. "I'd like to see more of your vision for the current residential buildings on the site before we move toward any major negotiations. Contact me when you've done that. Remember that many families have lived there for thirty years, and I don't plan on evicting them for anything."

A maybe instead of a yes or no. Roman wasn't quite sure how to feel about it. He was so used to the clear-cut response of one or the other, but this limbo state made him sit back a moment.

"Okay, I can get to work on that." He stuffed several papers back into his briefcase and placed his napkin on his empty dessert plate. "I'll have some drawings made of our vision and contact you with them."

"I'll be gone the rest of this week, but I'm available most of next."

The two men stood, each extending a hand. They shook over the table, and Roman nodded. "I'll make sure to have everything drawn up and ready for Monday morning, then."

Silvain grinned. "Anxious, are we?"

Roman shook his head and laughed. "I'd just like to get my job done as soon as possible to allow for my team to take it over and make the details come to life."

They both walked out the door of the restaurant, and Roman turned, ready to walk back to his hotel, when the older man spoke again. "Please don't worry about your father's debt. It's not yours to settle."

Without another word, the man turned and walked in the opposite direction, leaving Roman standing with his mouth open in the middle of the pavement.

Emotion filled him. He'd never felt such forgiveness as this man had just given. Everyone had always scrutinized him as though he were the clone of his father, down to his criminal activity. To have someone who'd been the victim of his father's schemes extend a small olive branch, it helped soothe more of the pain than he'd realized he'd been carrying around.

Finally moving, he walked back to his hotel. Pulling out his phone, he called Sam. "Prepare the plane. I need to get back to London as soon as possible. I have a contract to win."

CHAPTER 10

The next few days were a little crazy as Isabelle worked to fulfill her job with Darcy during the day and then made arrangements for the town house at night.

Her apartment was covered in magazines and sample pieces, with a vision board clustered with the ideas she'd come up with. Caren, her roommate, wasn't pleased with the mess, but at this point, Isabelle knew this project could be a turning point in her career, and maybe even her life. If that were the case, maybe she wouldn't have to endure the girl's pointed looks anymore.

She'd picked out the paint colors and carpet on Saturday, which allowed the painting crew time to get working on her unit early Monday morning. She'd been working on the elements for the town house for the last few hours, doing her best to track everything down and hopefully get it all in one trip. How she was going to get it all there, she still hadn't worked that out. But if Roman had given her his credit card with no questions asked, he probably wouldn't mind her taking some kind of company vehicle to pick up everything she'd need.

Dialing a number on the file, she pulled out the list of things she still needed to do.

"Hello." A deep voice came through the line.

Isabelle pulled up the screen with the chair she'd been eyeing for the past hour, trying to decide if it would work in the space. "Hello. I need to buy the gray wingback chair you have on special right now."

"I think you called the wrong number for that, Isabelle." The voice on the other line chuckled, and Isabelle pulled her phone away to look at the screen. She'd dialed Roman.

Giggling, she said, "Well, I needed to talk to you anyway, so that works. Too bad you don't have that chair in stock so I could be done with two calls at once." She grinned, waiting for his response.

"Well, at least you needed to talk to me. What's up?"

Going down the list with her finger, she stopped where it said *hardware.*

"Okay, I've been looking at the knobs for all of the cabinets throughout the units, and while the basic ones will do the job, I think the ones that are a little more expensive will make the place stand out a bit more. It's a subtle thing, and if you don't want to spend the extra—"

"Isabelle, it's fine. I trust you on it." His words sank deep into her chest as a feeling of comfort spread throughout her body. It wasn't often she'd had the trust of someone so quickly, and it was a new experience.

"Thanks. Okay, so far I've got most of the furniture coming in Friday. I should be done with the project with Darcy by then, and I'll have enough time to get everything set up before the open house on Saturday. Does that work?"

Roman cleared his throat. "That's fine with me. Will you

have any time in there to rest? It sounds like staging will take all night."

"It usually does when I'm with Darcy anyway." Isabelle leaned back in her chair and closed her eyes, knowing the week ahead was going to be exhausting but worth it. "We start staging for a house on Wednesday, and I'm hoping to finish by Thursday night."

"We can push off the open house if you want. I don't want you catching a cold." The tone of his voice was soft, sending another wave of butterflies flitting through her insides.

Isabelle clicked onto her calendar on the computer and shook her head. "No, let's just get it done this weekend. I'd prefer Darcy didn't find out I'm working with you on this, and the sooner we can do it, the fewer people will know."

"Okay. I'll see if I can stop over and help out." There was a pause on the other line, and then he said, "Isabelle, I've got to run, but keep me updated on anything you need this week."

"Will do. Thanks."

She hung up the phone, satisfied things were going in the right direction. This was the perfect plan, trying out her own business while still having a job. It gave her a sense of freedom as she didn't feel belittled by every decision. And it wasn't the worst thing to work with an attractive real estate agent either.

THE WEEK FLEW by as she and Darcy prepared to stage a large house on the outskirts of London. Isabelle did all she could to keep her mouth shut and work hard, knowing she'd be able to work on her own project soon enough.

She and Darcy had everything arranged just so by Thursday night. Friday morning, Isabelle could feel a cold creeping into her body. Her throat was on fire, and every part of her sinuses ached.

After the fourth time Isabelle coughed in the office next to Darcy's, she heard her boss's voice call out, "That is disgusting." Within seconds, Darcy stomped over to Isabelle's desk, stopping several feet away. "If you're going to keep coughing and sneezing, you may as well leave for the day. I don't want germs on all of the samples."

Isabelle nodded, pulling her purse out of the desk drawer. "Thanks, Darcy."

"Don't thank me. You won't be paid for the hours you miss." Turning on her heel, Darcy moved back to her desk.

Rolling her eyes, Isabelle left the office, frustrated at the fact that Darcy was garnishing her wages when she was the one sending Isabelle home.

She wanted nothing more than to go to bed and sleep for a few days. But the extra few hours would help get things organized how she envisioned, so she took a bus to the town house instead.

Walking in the front door, she was grateful to see all of the things she'd ordered stacked against one wall. After talking to Roman earlier in the week about borrowing a car, he insisted she have everything sent to his offices and he would make sure they were delivered.

"Here goes nothing," she said, opening the first box. She just hoped she'd be able to make it through the night so she could recover before Monday. Missing another day of work would bring suspicion, and she still didn't like the thought of being jobless.

rriving at the town houses on Friday evening, Roman was surprised to find a couple of furniture delivery trucks parked along the curb. He opened the front door and slipped inside, having to edge around a large couch that looked like it hadn't been arranged yet. A large pile of boxes sat against one wall, the inside bubble wrap and packing paper piled high next to it. Lamps and other knick-knacks were sitting out front as if Isabelle had unpacked everything and then disappeared to work on something in the unit.

What was she going to do with all this stuff? The fact that he'd actually hired someone to stage the place still made him chuckle a bit, but he had to admit, she was right about the color of paint on the walls, as well as the mixed color of the carpet.

Ducking his head into the kitchen, there was no sign of her, so he walked to the master bedroom. He almost walked back out, when he heard some rustling coming from the master bathroom. He peeked around the corner and saw

Isabelle using one of those releasable hooks to hang a small watercolor.

"Quite the operation you've got going on here," he said.

She jumped and turned to him, her hand on her chest as she tried to breathe.

Roman chuckled, sticking his hands in his pockets. "I'm sorry. I didn't mean to scare you."

"You're fine. I was just in my own little world back here." She walked toward him, and he moved back to let her pass. "What do you think so far?"

Roman scrunched his face to emphasize he was thinking. "I like the carpet. It's comfortable. That seems like a lot of stuff out front, but I trust you."

She stood with her hand on her hip, her eyes narrowed as she stared at him. "And what makes you trust me?"

It was the most intense stare he'd seen from her, and the dark blue of her eyes seemed to draw him in even further, tugging on a feeling he couldn't yet place.

"Instinct. Besides, I figured if you don't usually get to do this with your own ideas, you'll probably give this chance 110%. Is there anything I can do to help you?"

Roman didn't have the slightest idea of what he would have to do. His own apartment had been decorated by his cousin when she'd been trying to start her own design business. Now that she lived in LA, he'd heard she'd been doing quite well for herself.

Thinking about her made him wonder what took him so long to use a stager for his apartments and houses. He'd always gotten plenty of compliments when he had company over.

"Do you have time?" She looked at him with an odd expression.

Looking down at his watch, he saw that it was already

eight. "Yeah, I don't have much else going on except sleeping at some point. But I feel bad doing even that if you're going to be up all night."

She shrugged her shoulders and then pinched the bridge of her nose. "I'm used to this. Although, I've never done two projects so close together, and my throat is on fire. I'll probably be here all night, but I'll take as much help as you're willing to give."

"I'm actually more curious than I thought I'd be. Put me to work!" He gave her a wide grin, and she answered him back with one.

"Okay, I'll need you to put those sheets," she pointed to a package on the floor a few feet away, "on this bed, and then the comforter set is…" She paused a minute as she looked around the room. Her eyes locked onto something. She pointed and said, "That package behind the nightstand has all of the bedding. Just channel your inner maid to make sure it's nice and neat."

Roman nodded, chuckling at her words as she turned to walk back into the bathroom. He was beginning to like this girl with her quirky ways and down-to-earth personality. It had been a long time since he'd known anyone like her, as he'd done a lot of hiding in the past few years, and he realized how refreshing it was. The fact that she didn't focus on his scar and treated him like a normal human again reminded him that maybe there was life outside of work.

That feeling in his chest tugged a bit more, and he got to work, knowing he wouldn't be helping her by standing there all night.

Shaking his head, he pulled out the teal sheets, tugging them to fit around the king-size mattress. The headboard was tufted and a dark gray, and once he'd placed the navy-blue comforter set on the bed, he was amazed at how much the colors popped against the freshly painted sage wall. If this was just the beginning of the transformation of this apartment, he couldn't wait to see it all put together.

CHAPTER 12

The sound of a door opening caused Isabelle to jerk awake. The last thing she remembered, she'd sat down to get a better idea of what to do next, and now she could see the beginnings of morning shining in the sky. Her heart raced as she realized she hadn't locked the door the night before after Roman left.

Picking up a lamp, she poised it over her shoulder while hiding against a wall and waiting.

When Roman appeared around the corner, she breathed a sigh of relief, and amusement played on his lips.

"What were you going to do with that?" he asked, pointing to the lamp in her hands. "Did I scare you?"

She set down the lamp and rubbed her eyes. "I fell asleep, and when I heard the door, my mind started creating possibilities of someone breaking in."

She looked at him dressed in a navy-blue suit with a coral tie, and her stomach flipped. Man, he was attractive in a suit and always seemed to be so well put together. She ran a hand through her hair, her insides sinking as she realized what she must look like after a night of staging.

A smirk played on his lips. "I'm glad you decided I wasn't worth attacking. You had a serious face that would've scared anyone off."

"You have an expression that can do that as well. I can see why people rush around at your beck and call."

Roman looked as though he were considering something, a deep crease in his forehead. "Are you saying I'm scary?" His eyes were curious, the corner of his mouth inching up a bit.

"Not to me, no, but I can see how people would think that when you scowl. Like the day on the bus, with your dark green eyes and frown."

"And scar?" The words were little more than a whisper, but they were filled with pain.

Shaking her head, Isabelle said, "No. I think the scar brings out your cheekbones. To me, it makes you look like you've been through a lot but still won whatever battle you were waging."

Roman's eyes narrowed, and after several seconds of keeping his eye contact, Isabelle glanced away, feeling the butterflies and bees and every flying insect possible flying around in her stomach. She needed to get a grip.

Looking at the clock she'd hung on the wall a few hours before, she turned back and asked, "What are you doing here this early? It's only six in the morning."

He held out a large bottle of orange juice, and she took it from him, taking a few seconds to twist off the cap. The juice soothed her aching throat, and she took several gulps. When she brought the bottle back down, she saw a small bag in his hand and looked at it curiously. She smelled something freshly baked, and her stomach responded with a loud growl.

Roman held out the bag, and she took it, peeking inside. "I got a crêpe for you. I figured you'd be hungry after the long night. I debated whether to get you tea or coffee, but I remembered you saying your throat hurt and figured an orange juice might help with that for a bit. At least to get you through the last few hours here."

"Thank you. That means a lot." Shucking off her shoes, Isabelle moved out to the couch in the living room and sat down, pulling her legs underneath her as she pulled the crêpe out of the bag. It wasn't as good as the ones from back home in France, but with not much in her system from the day before, she wasn't going to complain.

Roman moved to the love seat across from her, placing his arm on the armrest. He sipped from his cup, staring at her with those piercing green eyes.

She glanced around the room. "What do you think so far?" She took a bite of the crêpe, chewing slowly as she waited for his answer.

"It looks really good, completely different to how it did before. Good choice on colours." He paused a moment and turned his attention back to her. "How long have you been staging?"

"About three years. I started with Darcy when I applied after an internship. I couldn't believe my luck at first. Now I feel like I haven't progressed as much as I should have after all this time."

"Did you like your internship?"

Isabelle nodded, swallowing a gulp of orange juice. "I loved it. Trisha was really good at her job, a real people person. She taught me all the basics, but she only takes interns, so when I found out about getting the job with Darcy, she was so excited for me." She leaned her head back on the couch, remembering. "I was ecstatic going into Stewart Design, excited to bring new ideas and to learn from her. But…" She let her voice trail off as she mentally reviewed some of the worst moments in her time with Darcy.

"But what?" Roman had his head turned slightly as if trying to hear better.

Shaking her head, Isabelle shrugged. "I don't know. I just haven't felt that creative since I've been with her. Until now, that is." She motioned to all the stuff around her. "This has been incredible, and whether or not I pass your test, it was a good wake-up call."

"So, do you think you'll quit?" She was surprised by the curiosity in his voice, as though he didn't make major decisions every day. From all of the properties with the Magnolia Property Group around London, she knew there was a lot that went into such a large company.

"No, not yet. I think I need a little more confidence in myself as a businesswoman before I can venture out on my own."

She took the last bite of crêpe and washed it down with a swig of orange juice. Setting the bottle on the coffee table in front of her, she stood and moved to grab some of the lap blankets from the small pile still left to distribute around the house. She threw one over the back of a small rocking chair and another over the long couch to match the blanket she'd placed on the love seat the previous evening. Pulling a bowl from one of the few boxes still in the room, she added some little knickknacks and set it on the table. After piling several books together, she walked them over to the shelves she'd ordered and stacked a few on each shelf.

When she turned, she saw Roman nodding off, his head jerking back every so often as it lowered toward his lap. He finally shifted his weight, sliding down with his head on the armrest.

Isabelle smiled and waited a few minutes, finishing off the shelves before she moved to his side.

Soft snores escaped his mouth and nose, and she lifted each of his legs onto the couch as softly as she could, hoping not to wake him. When he stopped moving, she pulled one of the blankets from the back of the love seat and laid it over him. When she moved away, she bumped the bowl on the coffee table as she walked by, causing one of the twine balls to roll underneath the couch.

She knelt to retrieve the ball, and as she looked up, she gazed at Roman's face, his sleeping form looking calm and collected. His defined jaw and light brown hair only accentuated the handsomeness of his face, as did the pink scar to the side. She'd seen him touch it often and wondered if it bothered him. She smiled as she felt the truth of her words earlier. It added to his features, emphasizing those gorgeous green eyes.

Butterflies took off inside her, and she shook her head. She looked down at the ring on her hand, wondering if it was time to take it off. From the intense feelings she had every time she was around Roman, she wondered if she'd ever loved Aaron at all. Her feelings for him were basic, more of a crush than love.

But Roman was her boss. For this job at least.

She stood, resuming the decorating. She still had quite a lot to do and couldn't stand around staring at the sleeping man on the couch any longer.

CHAPTER 13

Sunlight streamed in from the windows, one enthusiastic beam causing Roman to open his eyes. Feeling like he was coming out of a fog, he looked around, not knowing where he was. He sat up and whipped his head back and forth, trying to remember what had happened.

He took in the furniture and decor around him, reminding him he was at the town house. How had he fallen asleep? It had been a long week with a lot of late nights, but he'd come to help Isabelle with the last few items, not to be a sleeping lump she had to work around.

Standing up, he folded the blanket and tried to set it on the back of the love seat like Isabelle had done the night before. Looking around, he was amazed at the difference and the homely feel of the apartment. Maybe she needed to come and redo his own apartment, change out the modern décor for something that felt more like home.

He walked into the kitchen, hoping to find Isabelle hadn't slipped out. For some reason, he wanted to spend more time with her than ever, and after all she'd done to transform this unit, he knew he'd need to hire her to continue working for him on future projects. The idea thrilled him as he would be able to see her again.

He found her arranging a few items in the master bedroom and picking up some rubbish from the floor.

She turned around and jumped when she saw him standing there. With a mischievous smile, she said, "Looks like Prince Charming finally decided to wake up."

Prince Charming. It had been quite some time since he'd been called that. Definitely not since the accident. Was she trying to play with him? Or did she really mean it?

"Sorry. I've been working to get a proposal done, and I guess I'm more tired than I thought. What can I do?" He put his hands out before him, trying to emphasize he could do whatever she needed.

"I'm actually just picking up the last bit of garbage, and then I'll be ready to go. I could use some medicine and a long nap." She smiled, but he could hear the hoarseness in her voice.

"Why don't you head home? I can get it all cleaned up and ready for the open house. We've still got two hours until the open house begins, and it looks like you've already done the bulk of it."

Her eyebrow raised. "Are you sure? You're paying me to do this."

"You've done all the hard stuff already. It won't be that hard to put the garbage in the dumpster outside."

The smile she gave him made his knees buckle, and he was glad he was leaning against the doorframe.

After giving him a few instructions, one of which included him baking cookies, she moved to the front door and picked up her purse. "Thank you. I really appreciate it."

"How are you going to get home? Do you want me to call my driver?"

Isabelle laughed, the sound coming out like a croaking frog. "No. I think I'll go get a taxi on the next street over."

"Text me when you get home."

Why had he said that? They weren't dating. She was his subcontractor, and she was engaged. Or was she? He hadn't gotten the chance to ask, and now seemed awkward as she was out the door. Later. He'd ask her later. There was still a lot to prepare for the open house, and that needed to be his main focus now.

She gave him a small smile. "Will do."

That tug pulled in his chest, and he realized his feelings were growing for the French stager.

CHAPTER 14

*A*fter making a few calls, Roman was surprised to find it was almost noon. He'd given Shirley the assignment to get the word out about the open house over the past few days, and as people started to file in a few minutes before noon, he knew she needed a raise.

Roman set a plate of cookies he'd made from a store-bought packet on the island of the kitchen and leaned against it. He hadn't burned them, which was probably a good thing. Isabelle's idea had sounded ridiculous when she'd mentioned it, but now he understood that it added another layer of home to the homely atmosphere in the unit.

"Welcome, folks. Please let me know if you have any questions. Take a look around. We have several of these units for sale, some will be left undone for the buyers to pick paint and carpet, just for you to think about." The people nodded, looking surprised at the thought, and it made him wonder why he always rushed to have everything complete before an open house.

Isabelle had said something about letting people have options, and maybe that was a small change he could make in the company. With the option to choose some of the little details, it would give buyers the feel they wanted without overwhelming them by some of the bigger decisions that went into constructing a home. It was something to keep in mind for any new construction projects in the future.

After answering questions a younger couple had about the properties, Roman looked up at the large crowd milling through the town house. He couldn't believe how well things had gone so far. He'd known the basics of real estate development from a young age and had plenty of experiences with it after his time at Hawthorne, although it hadn't been his first choice of career. But even with all of the deals he'd made during the past five years as CEO of Magnolia Property Group, he'd never seen such a response.

Thirty minutes into the open house, he'd given out all of his business cards and even the few he had for Shirley in his wallet. She could have one of the newer agents help her get paperwork lined up for the ones who wanted to buy.

He thought of Isabelle and wanted to call her right then, but he pulled back, knowing she would probably be trying to recuperate after a long few days.

A woman walked up to him just then, her head tipped back with her nose in the air. She reached below his shoulders, causing her to crane her neck to look up at him. "May I ask who staged this apartment?"

Roman frowned, wary of the tightness of the woman's face. She looked familiar, liked he'd seen or met her recently, but he couldn't pinpoint where at the moment. "We hired someone to help us out with it. Why? Are you interested in hiring her for your own space?"

The woman narrowed her brown eyes, flipping a piece of her short dark-brown hair out of her face, and pursed her lips before saying, "I'm just surprised you didn't go with my firm for something like this." She waved her hands as she looked around the room. "I am one of the leading interior designers and stagers in the London area. Soon to be in Europe after a few projects finish in some other cities. I'm usually asked to at least give a bid for jobs like this."

"Excuse me," Roman said, trying to pull back from barking at her. "With your current attitude, I'm glad I didn't contact you."

Her jaw went slack and she said, "I apologize, Mr...?"

"Roman Hamilton. CEO of Magnolia. And yours?"

"Darcy Stewart." She said the words as if hesitant to reveal her identity.

Roman's stomach dropped. He recognized her face from the picture on her website. Isabelle's boss.

"It was a nice touch with the cookies. As far as I know, I'm the only staging company who uses that tactic." Her eyes narrowed, and Roman hoped she wasn't putting the pieces together that her employee had been the one to work on the home.

Doing his best to mask his realization, he nodded and stretched out his hand. "It's nice to meet you. Honestly, this is my first time working with staging and interior design, and I didn't even think to find a firm that does such things. Will you leave me your card so I can contact you for future jobs?"

Her lips went up at the corners only slightly as she opened her clutch and pulled out a pale-pink business card. "I would appreciate that greatly, sir. We have one of the best reputations around and would love to start working with your company."

He could see pound signs in her eyes, and as much as he wanted to put her in her place again, he knew the hope of a call from him would haunt her longer than a few disparaging words.

They nodded to each other as she walked out the door. Once she was out of sight, Roman picked up his phone, ready to compose a message to Isabelle. No, it would be better to call her in warning. He had to let her know that her little secret from Darcy was most likely no longer that.

Just as he'd found her name in his contacts and started to call, a young couple came up to him, asking several questions. Putting his phone in his back pocket, he turned to the couple, giving them his full attention as he worked his selling magic.

As the last few people were leaving the apartment, his phone rang, and he saw Shirley's name come up.

"I hope you're done at the open house. I don't think your plans for Monsieur Guilbert's property will live up to his expectations."

Irritation flashed through Roman, not happy about her words. She tended to be more blunt than most of his employees, and he was usually grateful for that. But there was something about wanting to celebrate today, and the thought that he just had more work to do made it difficult to get too excited.

"What don't you think he'll like?" Roman said after pausing to gain control of his voice, stripping it of frustration as much as possible.

"You told me it needed to be something for families and to accommodate the families currently living there while under construction. Your ideas make it look too modern, which isn't always practical for families."

Gritting his teeth, Roman called up a picture of his design in his mind. She had a point, but he wasn't happy about it. "What do you suggest I change?"

"Maybe get your stager to take a look at the plans. I'm sure she'll have a good idea of how to help you."

Running a hand through his hair, panic hit him in the gut. He'd never had a chance to warn Isabelle. "I'll call her. She might be needing a permanent job now anyway."

CHAPTER 15

Isabelle woke up late Saturday night, feeling as if she'd been hit by a truck. Her whole head felt stuffed, and breathing was near impossible through her nose.

She shuffled into the kitchen, grateful for the silence of the apartment. Her roommate was probably out with her group of friends, and Isabelle hoped she didn't come home anytime soon. The pounding in her head was enough against the quiet, and her roommate tended to be loud and obnoxious when drunk.

After heating some water in a kettle, she placed a bag of herbal tea in a cup and poured the water over it, pushing it down several times to steep. She hoped it would help.

She picked up her phone from where she'd left it on the table next to her bag. Pushing it on, she saw several missed calls from Roman and Darcy. What would both of them need? Had something gone wrong with the open house? And had some random item not come in that Darcy needed immediately?

Dialing the voice mail, Isabelle entered her password and heard the automated system tell her she had four new voicemails. The first was short and from Darcy, her words rough and angry.

"Please call me immediately. I have several things I need to discuss with you, and the longer you wait, well, let's just say you don't want to wait too long." It clicked, and the automated voice came on again.

Isabelle pushed delete, her heart pounding in her ears.

She waited for the next message to play, and Darcy's voice came on the line again. "I expect my employees to have the utmost respect for me and my company. I still have not heard from you. Call me." From the time it had been sent, it was only ten minutes after the first message.

Dread filled Isabelle's stomach, and from the shrill voice on Darcy's next message, she knew things weren't looking good for her employment status. "How dare you take a staging assignment behind my back. You are an employee of this company, and as such, all offers should be directed through me. The Hamiltons are billionaires, and something like this would put Stewart Design down as an international design company. You are fired!" The time for that message had come in only three minutes after the second.

She barely registered the fact that she'd been fired as her mind focused on *The Hamiltons are billionaires*. She only knew one billionaire, Tristan, and while he was a nice guy, the idea of that many zeroes in his bank account was still mind-boggling.

The information had trouble sinking into her brain. If Roman really was a billionaire, he was a lot different than Aaron, even though Aaron wasn't even close to that net worth. At least Roman didn't flaunt it, which was probably why she couldn't believe it.

Pressing delete to the two messages she'd just listened to as thoughts churned in her mind, she prepped herself for another lashing over voicemail, grateful she was getting the news like this instead of in person. Tears beaded up as she realized her worst fear had just been confirmed. Had Roman left a voicemail telling her that her design for the town house had tanked?

Roman's voice hit her ears with its deep baritone timbre, and she felt her shoulders relax somewhat. Whatever hole she'd dug by accepting the side job with him seemed to lose some of the gravity, helping her as she listened to his words.

"Isabelle, I'm sorry to tell you this, and I hope it's not too late. Your boss stopped by the open house, and I think she knows you're the one who worked on it. I was going to call you before but had some people with questions and didn't get a chance until now. Call me. I'd like to discuss how the open house went."

Ending the call, Isabelle picked up her tea and moved to the couch, sinking into the side where the couch swallowed her, helping ease some of the aches she now felt throughout her body. Taking a sip of the warm liquid, she felt it soothe her throat and trickle down to her stomach, easing some of the knots that had formed over the last few minutes.

After a few more minutes, she dialed Roman, deciding to get the bad news over with first. She already knew she was fired from Darcy's firm, so anything the woman had to say next wouldn't make much of an impact on her.

He picked up after one ring and said, "Isabelle. I'm glad you called. How are you feeling?"

"Sick," she said flatly. "I got your message. And Darcy's messages as well."

"I'm so sorry, Isabelle. I was trying to reach you to warn you about it. What did she say?" She heard a softness in his voice, like when she talked to her parents or people she loved. What could have prompted that? Maybe he just felt sorry for her.

"Well, she said a lot of things, but the most important one

is that I'm fired." She took a sip of her tea before asking, "How did the open house go?" Everything inside her tightened, the suspense of not knowing making it difficult to concentrate on anything else.

Roman chuckled a bit and finally said, "It went so well. We already have five offers, as well as several people who are interested in looking at some of the unfinished units. I took your advice and told a bunch of the visitors that we could change paint colors and carpet if they desired, and you should have seen their eyes light up."

Isabelle smiled, glad something in her life had gone right for once. "I'm surprised you haven't encountered that before with all of the projects you've done." As she said it, Darcy's words, *The Hamiltons are billionaires*, ran through her mind. She still couldn't wrap her head around it.

Before she could think about it too much, he said, "I do a lot of commercial properties and then buildings on a larger scale. This was an investment suggestion from one of my agents, and I'd begun to regret my impulse to buy it until you did all this work."

"Maybe your clients are just starstruck by your wealth and good looks and don't worry about those kinds of things until they move in." She took in a breath, waiting to see what he'd say. When he didn't reply, she continued. "In one of her messages, Darcy yelled at me that I'd ruined her chance with the Hamilton billionaires."

She heard a gasp on the other line before he said, "I doubt it's wealth or looks, to be honest. And like anyone, I'm still a human, no matter what my income looks like."

"I agree to that. I wish all people with money thought that way."

The line went silent for a few seconds before he said, "Now that you don't have a job, would you accept one with my company? Or at least allow me to hire you as a subcontractor?"

Part of her momentary depression lifted, the worry over what she would do next gone as she now had options. She could work full time for a large real estate firm, something Darcy had dreamed of ever since Isabelle had gone to work for her. The alternative would be to form her own company and be a subcontractor for Roman. Either decision sounded better than another three years with Darcy, but as she thought about it, she wanted the freedom to work as she pleased, without someone constantly watching over her shoulder. Not that Roman would necessarily do that, but she still liked the idea of her own company.

"I think I'll take a crack at creating a business. But I'd love to be your main subcontractor." She couldn't hide the excitement in her voice as she giggled. What were the odds that she'd create such a connection with a handsome man like Roman Hamilton?

"Great. Well, I have a task I need your help for as soon as you feel up to it. I was supposed to meet a man called Silvain Guilbert on Monday to give him a proposal for his property. Shirley doesn't think the layout and my ideas would work for the man's vision, and I thought you might be able to add some insight. I'll push off the meeting until later in the week?" His voice sounded so hopeful, and Isabelle couldn't help but smile. She could picture his face, his green eyes pleading, tearing down any hope she had of refusing him.

"Sure. Let me get some things figured out for my company, and I'll meet at your office Monday afternoon. If you email what you have now, I can take a look at them tomorrow while I'm recovering from this cold."

Roman was quiet a moment. "I could bring them over if you need anything else. Chicken soup? Medicine?"

"I'll be fine. I think I just need to rest."

"You know my number if you change your mind." She could tell he was smiling as he said the words, and her stomach felt like it was on a rollercoaster as she realized he wanted to see her.

"Thank you, Roman. I'll see you soon."

Once she hung up, she held the phone against her chest, breathing shallowly, hoping she wouldn't wake up if this was all a dream.

CHAPTER 16

Feeling much better Monday morning, Isabelle tried to focus on what she'd need to get done in the coming week. The excitement she felt over starting her own company was still as strong as when she was talking to Roman Saturday night, but fear mixed in as she realized all that she would be responsible for. She just had to make sure it didn't turn her into Darcy in the long run.

She tried to pretend she hadn't been looking at her phone all weekend, hoping Roman's name would pop up with a phone call or text. Now that they would be working together often, she knew she needed to put some boundaries on her heart and make sure it didn't go crazy. She'd been dumped two weeks earlier, and there was no way she could jump into another relationship that quickly. As nice as Roman was to her, she still worried that when it came to a relationship outside of work, he'd turn into Aaron, claiming she wasn't good enough for his world.

Curiosity about Roman took her to type his name into a search engine, wondering if Darcy's words about him had been correct.

She looked at the top corner, and the first thing that caught her attention was how many search results there were, many with Roman's name in the short description, along with Magnolia Property Group. A picture finally loaded to the right, showing a picture of Roman without the long scar on his face. The picture made him look more arrogant than what she knew of the man she'd been working with the past week, and she wondered if the accident had changed him more than a scar on the face and a fear of driving on the roads.

Clicking on the first link, she waited as it loaded before scrolling down. She scanned the first couple of paragraphs until she saw Roman's name. It was an interview with him for a local real estate magazine.

I got into this business when things went south for my father. There were so many people already employed by Magnolia, and if I didn't step in to fix things, that many more people would have been out of jobs. We've made large strides in the few years I've been with the company, but the things we've been able to do as a group since then have made a great impact in many cities worldwide.

The article went on to state that Magnolia donated hundreds of thousands of pounds to charities in London, as well as some based in the US.

She clicked out of the article and refreshed the search with Roman's name in it. Wikipedia came up first, and her mouth dropped open as it stated he was one of the youngest billionaires in the world and the highest paid CEO for real estate development.

Of all the people she'd had the chance to meet, she was grateful she'd stumbled into Roman. If it weren't for him, she'd be running to get Darcy's specialty coffee this morning.

Opening her email, she saw one from Roman titled "Paris Property Specs."

Hey, Isabelle.

Thanks for checking this over for me. Silvain wants it to be appealing to families and workable for the current tenants. Any thoughts you have would be great.

Roman

Opening up the plans, she was surprised by how much they outlined the opposite of functionality for families. The kitchen layout didn't flow well with the rest of the floorplan.

Isabelle went back to her web browser and looked up some of the past properties represented by the Magnolia Group. There was quite a mixture from traditional to modern designs, and she wondered if all of those ideas had originated with Roman.

As she saw the property and what was around it, ideas flowed into her mind, and she started sketching them out on a smaller scale than the regular plans. After another hour, she packed up all the information and drawings, ready to begin her first day as her own boss. She just hoped Roman was willing to listen to her advice.

* * *

Isabelle stopped at Stewart Design first thing that morning, hoping not to run into Darcy. Luck was not on her side as the woman sat behind her desk, scowling at Isabelle. Trying not to worry about her, Isabelle filled a box with her things and made sure to take everything off the computer that she needed.

She picked up the box and took a few steps toward the door, when Darcy's voice pierced the air.

"I'll make sure you don't work in this town again. Then others will know not to cross me."

Spinning around, Isabelle narrowed her eyes, now seeing the woman before her for exactly what she was: an insecure control freak.

"I'll make do. I love doing this, and all it takes is a couple of referrals to get something going. You taught me that." Isabelle smiled and turned back to the door, feeling a rush of adrenaline at the slack-jawed expression of her former boss.

Once she'd taken her box back to her place, the ride over to the Magnolia office building was uneventful in comparison, and Isabelle's brain wouldn't turn off with all the ideas flowing for the property she'd only seen on the screen. Walking through the doors, she moved to the reception desk.

"Hi," she said a bit nervously. Roman hadn't gone into the particulars for what she needed to do to go up, but it was always easier to start with the receptionist. "I need to speak with Roman Hamilton."

The woman smiled as she typed something into her computer. "Your name?"

"Isabelle Rousseau."

Glancing up, the woman nodded. "One moment, please. I'll call up to see if he's in." She picked up the handheld remote and spoke into the receiver. After explaining the situation, she nodded and said, "Thank you," before hanging up the phone.

"You can head up the elevators to your right. Just go to the twelfth floor."

Isabelle thanked the woman and walked over to the elevators.

There was such a different feeling from the first time she'd been there compared to now. That first time, it had sparked a sliver of hope that her life could change. Now, here she was, getting ready for her first meeting as her own boss and feeling totally out of her element. But Roman had faith in her and would hopefully guide her through the best practices for a newbie business owner.

Waiting by the elevators, she glanced around, something she hadn't done the last time she'd been there, taking in the modern look of the building and finishes. If he'd designed this building, there were going to be a lot of things she'd have to educate him on when it came to working with a person's home. It was one thing to make a building modern, but when it came time to go home to relax, it needed to be comfortable and befitting the inhabitants.

The elevator shifted open, and she walked in, trying to come up with things she could say. Would she be blunt and tell him the designs wouldn't work for what the client wanted? Or would she just go with his ideas?

The doors opened, and she stepped out, looking around. The simplicity of it all surprised her as it seemed so different from the ground floor. There weren't a ton of flourishes or extravagant art pieces like in the lobby. Maybe it was just her designer eye taking in everything from a new perspective that had her judging the office. The smell of cookies wafted to her, and her stomach grumbled. She'd gotten so caught up in the plans and the design that she'd forgotten to eat lunch.

"Are you Isabelle?" a woman behind a large desk stood and asked.

"Yes. I am here to—"

"Speak with Roman." Her face broke into a mischievous smile, and her tone sounded as though this happened every day. She held out her hand over the desk, and Isabelle shook it firmly. "I'm Shirley, Roman's assistant. Though I'm more of a lifeline than he'd like to admit." Her bright smile helped ease some of Isabelle's nervousness. For what, she didn't know just yet.

"It's good to meet you. I didn't get the chance when I was here before."

"I was probably out running an errand for Roman or fixing the printer. I swear that thing knows when I'm most busy and won't do anything I need it to in a timely manner."

The two women laughed, and Isabelle looked around to

see that Roman's office was empty, and disappointment settled in. "I take it he's not here right now." She motioned to the office.

Shirley turned to look and then looked back at her. "He just went to talk to one of the agents down the hall. Go on in and have a seat. Can I get you anything? Soda, water, coffee?"

Isabelle raised a hand and shook her head. "I'm fine, thank you."

"Are you feeling better, dear? Roman said you'd worked so hard you got a cold. I can't believe you're here right now. You'll need more time to rest if you're going to work with him." She winked at Isabelle, and the younger woman wasn't sure how to feel about it.

With her mouth agape, Isabelle studied the woman, trying to figure out something underlying the words. "He talked about me? I barely know him."

"But you pulled off something great enough to shock him, so I wouldn't be too surprised. Besides, you're the first woman he's mentioned more than once in one day in the last five years, so count yourself lucky." Shirley gave her a knowing smile.

Isabelle shook her head. "We're not—"

"Not what?" Roman's voice asked over her shoulder.

She spun to face him, feeling the heat rushing to her cheeks. "Nice to see you too," she said with sarcasm, hoping to avoid explaining what Shirley had revealed to her.

Roman smiled, the dimple appearing and causing her heart to skip a beat. "It's good to see you looking better. Come in, and we'll discuss the plans."

Isabelle nodded, entering Roman's office with a few quick steps, ready to get rid of the crazy feelings racing through her. Sure, she was attracted to the man before her, but she shouldn't be thinking that. Shirley's words just made it that much harder to get out of her head. It wasn't as though the woman had stated that Roman liked Isabelle as more than a colleague, but the insinuation was there.

Taking a seat next to a small table by the window, Isabelle glanced to the landscape below, comforted by the serenity of the scene. Turning back, she saw Roman sitting in the chair next to her, studying her face with a neutral expression.

Isabelle took that as a cue to begin and pulled her drawings out from her bag. "I took some time to look over these this morning." Now was the moment of truth. "I think these plans miss the vision of the client. It's all modern. It might be nice for some clients, but the majority of families need something functional that helps with everyday life." She paused, looking up to see his reaction.

Roman nodded and leaned forward, pulling one of Isabelle's drawings toward him. "What have you changed in these?" He pointed to her sketches and looked up at her, raising his eyebrows.

Leaning closer, Isabelle got a whiff of his cologne, the smell of sandalwood mesmerizing her for a few seconds. Avoiding eye contact with Roman, she pointed out different features she'd envisioned.

"Opening up this wall will give the small rooms a larger feel. Everyone talks about open concept these days, but it helps to allow more space for bigger families, or even someone who likes to have company."

Pointing to one section, he said, "So this wall that separates the entry from the kitchen and family room will be gone?"

Isabelle nodded. "There are a lot of ways to section off the rooms without a wall, and a lot of people like that flexibility."

He sat back in the chair, staring out the window. He cupped his chin with his hand and rubbed his fingers against the small hairs that had already grown out this late in the day. Several seconds passed with him not saying a word, and

Isabelle organized the papers, trying to keep her mind busy. She just hoped she hadn't screwed up her first test as a business owner.

When he finally spoke, it was with that deep voice, and Isabelle was grateful she was sitting down. As much as she wanted to keep things professional, the little things kept tantalizing her. But she was newly single after a rough breakup. She didn't want a rebound guy. Or so she kept trying to tell herself.

"I think your vision will work for the client. Can you do a more formal drawing of this if I send you the plans? We can set up a computer here with the programs to do so if you need it." His green eyes stared into her own, and she could feel her heart rate speed up a notch.

Swallowing with some effort, she said, "I think I'll be fine. I have some software on my computer at home."

He bent over the table, only inches from her face. "How long do you think it will take to finalize?"

Isabelle broke her gaze from his, taking in a breath to refocus. Glancing down at the plans, she said, "A day, maybe two."

"Okay, I'll make arrangements to fly to Paris on Thursday. I'd like you to come with me if you don't mind. I think your description of what we'll do to the property will help sway the man to sell it to us."

Placing a hand on her chest, she asked, "You want me to come with you? Are you sure about that?"

One side of Roman's mouth turned up, and a chuckle came from deep inside him. "After a presentation like that, it should be you and not me telling him about it. Besides, this could be a way to get more business. Silvain Guilbert owns a lot of property and has a lot of pull in Paris."

Isabelle's stomach fell, disappointment seeping through.

"You don't think I'll be busy enough working for your company?"

"Oh, I can keep you busy. I just thought you might like to make those kinds of connections early on. It can help grow your business faster than you think." The look on his face was tender, the corners of his mouth turned up slightly.

It took the air out of her lungs as she realized how much she learned about him each time they were together. What kind of man would encourage her to do something to better herself and her business when it might affect his own? Not that he couldn't find a stager anywhere with his kind of money, but it was such a stark contrast to how Aaron would've acted.

"Thank you."

He nodded. "Well, can you fly with me?"

"Yeah, I think that will work out well. I'll book a seat when I get home." She stood, slipping the papers back into her bag and pulling the strap over her shoulder. Maybe she would stay an extra day and visit Juliette. It had been a while since they had spent the day together in Paris.

Roman stood as well, reaching out his hand and touching her arm. "Don't worry about that. I've hired you for this, and I'll handle the flight."

Isabelle's gaze flicked down to his lips, and she rolled her lips in, hoping it would curb the urge to lean forward and kiss him. Her mind willed her legs to walk toward the door, knowing that distance right now was for the best.

At the door, she said, "Okay, just let me know what time we'll be leaving."

Without waiting for an answer, she pushed her strides longer and longer until she arrived at the door to the stairs. Twelve floors were a lot to go down, but at that point, it would help her put her mind back into its safe space where it could guard her heart from further heartbreak.

CHAPTER 17

*R*oman had made arrangements with Isabelle to pick her up at six on Thursday morning, wanting to make sure they beat the morning traffic. Sam knew a lot of the backroads to get to the airstrip, but it was still easier to schedule flights out first thing in the morning so he didn't have to worry about the extra cars on the road.

They pulled up to the address she'd given him, and Sam put the limo in park before turning back to look at Roman. "Shall I go fetch her, sir?"

Roman shook his head. "No, I'll do it."

He climbed out of the car and quickstepped up the few stairs in front of the small building. Her flat was on the third floor, so he continued to walk up, feeling his breath quicken with the effort. Standing in front of 304, he knocked lightly, hoping she would be able to hear it. The door opened a crack just as his hand moved back to his side, and he jumped, surprised that she'd been right there.

Isabelle opened it wider, wheeling a suitcase out the door and grabbing a larger handbag from the coffee table. She smiled at him before turning to lock the door.

In a whisper, she said, "My roommate had another late night, and if we wake her up, my things would probably be in a box outside when I get back. It doesn't matter that she wakes me up almost every night she goes out. Oh well." She waved a hand like that was the end of it.

"That sounds like an adventure. My sisters wake me up, but that's because I threaten them if they don't. It's surprising how being stuck at home when their mates are out helps keep them in line." He grinned at her before lifting her bag and walking down the stairs. "What do you have in here?" he asked with a laugh.

"I like to be prepared. You said two days, but there are a ton of things that could happen or that we could do in that time. Yeah, we might be stuck in some office hashing things out to finalize the sale, but what if Mr. Guilbert wants us to meet his family or there's a spontaneous party near the Eiffel Tower?"

They'd reached the bottom of the stairs, and Roman turned to look at her, laughing harder than he had in a long time. "A spontaneous party by the Eiffel Tower? Is that your favorite place in Paris?"

She scrunched her nose and shook her head. "Are you kidding? I only go there when forced. It gets too many tourists. My favorite place is the Sacré-Cœur."

Roman nodded. "I think I've been there once. I don't get a lot of time to sightsee while I'm in Paris. It's usually negotiating with a client or visiting with one of my frat brothers."

Roman opened the door for Isabelle, and she got in. He handed her bag to Sam and climbed in, sitting a few inches away from her on the same back seat.

"Where did you go to school?" she asked, cocking her head to the side.

"Hawthorne University in California."

Isabelle's eyebrows drew together, and she looked at him

with her mouth open but nothing coming out. "Is your friend Tristan Delacroix?"

Smiling, Roman said, "Yeah. How'd you know?"

"He's dating my sister, Juliette. Well, practically engaged already."

Roman's jaw dropped open as he put all the pieces together. "I should have put that together before now. I guess I just figured it was a popular last name in France." He paused for a second. "Are you not happy about their relationship?"

Isabelle looked at her fingernails. "They're great together, almost too perfect. But after all Juliette went through in high school, she deserves a good guy. I guess I'm a little bit envious is all."

The sadness on her face pulled at Roman's chest, and he had to avoid the urge to lean over and gather her into his arms.

Looking down at the ring on her finger, he finally asked, "You don't have to answer if you don't want to, but are you engaged?"

Isabelle flexed her left hand and looked down at the ring, a cackle coming from her. "I was. He broke up with me a few days before our bus incident."

For a few seconds, Roman felt the excitement of knowing he wasn't developing feelings for someone who was off-limits completely. But those feelings were squashed as he realized she must still be hanging on to feelings for her ex-fiancé.

Turning to get a better look at her, he rested his arm on the back of the seat, sitting up so he could see her face clearly. "Why do you still wear it, then?"

She shrugged. "I don't really know. I've thought about taking it off in the past few days, but that's usually when I'm out doing something and don't have a safe place for it."

"Do you still love him?" The words sounded like rocks coming out of his mouth, and he tried to act casual, willing his face to relax.

"Now that we aren't together, I've realized he wasn't the guy I want to spend my life with, but it's just one more failure in my life. I guess the ring helps remind me not to get too stuck in my fantasy world and realize that life is nothing like the fairy tales."

"What makes you think you're a failure? Don't you remember that awesome open house you helped pull off? I would call that a major success."

A tear rolled down her cheek, and Roman reached up to wipe it away while steadying himself against the movement of the car. She gave him a smile and looked back down.

"My sister had major acne, like so bad that pictures of her back then compared to now are shocking. She started her own skin care line, and now she's this successful business owner. You went through a traumatic accident and have had to learn how to take care of your sisters when your father went to jail. What's my problem? I don't have major stumbling blocks in my way, and yet I feel like I can never measure up to everyone's expectations."

The fact that she'd included him in her short list made him swell with pride. He *had* gone through a lot in the last five years, and he'd never dared to hope that anyone would look at those events as if he'd overcome them.

Against his better judgment, Roman wrapped his arm around her shoulders and pulled her close, liking how she fit against him. Her light floral scent reached his nose, and he breathed in, trying to come up with something to make her feel better. That tug he'd been feeling for several days was pulling hard now, and he knew he had to help her through whatever it was she needed.

"Maybe that's the problem. You're trying to please everyone. What expectations do you have for yourself?"

"I don't know. I know I love staging and designing. I guess I just figured I'd be further along in my career by now."

"There's nothing wrong with starting today. There are so many people who weren't successful until much later in life. I'm talking fifties and sixties. You have so much before you, and you can build this company with your passion." He took in a breath and continued. "If I had a real passion for real estate, I can't imagine what would happen."

She sat up, wiping at the moisture on her cheeks. "You don't like real estate? But you're a gazillionaire. You can't tell me you don't like it just a bit."

Roman laughed, the release feeling good for him, and she followed. "I like it, but it wasn't my first choice of professions. I always wanted to write books or invent something that would change the course of the world. But I didn't want the company to tank altogether, and I'm good at it. I can negotiate with some of the toughest people out there, but sometimes I just need backup." He pointed to her and nodded.

The limo stopped, and Sam opened the door. Roman helped Isabelle out of the car and walked around to grab her bag.

"Wait!"

Her loud voice caused him to turn, worried that something might be wrong. "What's wrong?"

She pointed toward the luxury plane sitting before them. "We're not at the regular airport! Are we flying in that?"

Roman smiled and nodded, enjoying the bewildered expression on her face. "The company owns the plane."

"You mean you own the plane." She raised her eyebrows as if to signal not to challenge her.

"Maybe. But it's nice to not have to move through all the people."

Sam shut the trunk and said, "We should probably get going. It looks like it might rain soon, and I don't want to worry about anything while we're in the air."

CHAPTER 18

Sam's voice came over the speaker above to tell them they were only a few miles from the airport in Paris, and Isabelle couldn't get over the fact that she'd just flown in a private luxury plane. It had been everything she could have asked for, and when her chair leaned back enough to become a bed, she knew she was ruined from regular travel for the rest of her life. Not that the flight was that long, but she could imagine some of the longer flights being the opposite of stuffed in a can for several hours.

Roman sat his chair back up and smiled, his sleep-filled eyes almost closing with the action. "Are you ready?"

"As ready as I can be. How was your nap?"

"Good. Not long enough, but I'll survive."

Once they landed and parked the plane, the three of them walked to the hangar where a car sat waiting for them.

Looking in Roman's direction, she said, "Do you have cars at every airport?"

"No, just a few throughout Europe. The ones I do the most business with. It makes it easier to fly in and get to the destination. Car companies aren't always the most reliable at getting there when I need to hurry to a meeting."

They got in and drove the few miles to the property they would be negotiating. Isabelle looked at it, trying to cement a physical picture into her mind. With that image, she could mentally switch out things to help her with a design.

After circling the houses and industrial buildings, Sam parked the car at a small restaurant at the end of the property they were looking at. Everything was just on the edge of the city of Paris, but Isabelle had never been to this part before.

"What are we doing?" she asked Roman as she shifted her bag back onto her shoulder.

"Brunch with Mr. Guilbert." He smiled at her, but the action didn't reach his eyes. As he stepped out of the car, she saw a tightness in his features and upper body. Was he nervous?

He reached for her hand to help her out, sending prickles of electricity zinging down her arm again. Why did he have such an effect on her?

They started walking toward the restaurant, and he didn't let go of her hand, increasing his grip tighter with each step like she was a lifeline to something. She didn't mind, but it was sending her nervous system into overdrive. It didn't help her brain, either, as she tried to figure out how she was feeling about the whole situation.

Opening the door, they walked in, and Roman led her over to a larger man with white hair sitting at a table near the corner. The two of them shook hands, and Isabelle hung back, not sure what she should do at that point.

Roman turned and pointed to her, his other hand resting on the small of her back, and had she not needed to be professional at that moment, she might have turned around and kissed him. Aaron had never done something as simple or as intimate as that, and the fact that Roman had when they weren't even dating made her swoon.

"So, Isabelle the stager. You come from the right country, huh?" The teasing expression on the man's face made her laugh.

Glancing up at Roman, she smiled and said, "Yes, I am French. My family is from Dinan."

"Ahh, beautiful country. I don't get up to Brittany often enough, but I think I'll have to make a special trip now, at least to meet the parents of such a beautiful young lady."

Isabelle could feel the heat creep into her cheeks at the man's words.

"Well, have a seat, you two," Silvain said. "Let's get things started here. We'll have some food brought out in a moment so we can eat and talk business. There's no better middle ground than at the table."

Roman rolled out a set of plans he'd brought in a large tube. Isabelle recognized the different sheets as the ones she'd spent the last couple of days designing and rolled her lips in, hoping this meeting would go as well as Roman hoped it would. His body was still tense, as if ready to flee if given the opportunity.

A young man brought in several platters of food, and Silvain waved his hand over them, telling Roman and Isabelle to eat up.

Isabelle pulled a croissant near her, as well as some fruit, grateful for something to settle her stomach. She'd been so nervous earlier that she'd forgotten to eat.

"What have you brought me, Roman?" Silvain murmured, slipping a pair of thin spectacles over his nose. He leaned forward, looking over the elements on the page, making little grunts every so often. Isabelle just hoped the sounds were positive.

Shocking even herself, Isabelle shifted over and placed

her hand into Roman's, squeezing a moment. He finally turned to her, his smile slight and a faraway look in his eyes. She moved to withdraw her hand, but he squeezed it, holding it in place. When she stopped trying to pull away, he relaxed his grip, and she tried to focus on the meeting before her, even though her insides were going crazy.

Silvain looked up. "Okay, what do we have here?"

She sensed Roman's hesitation and wondered what was so different about this situation versus all the negotiations he'd done before. Since he was a billionaire, he had to be successful at this.

When he didn't speak, she leaned forward, letting go of his hand. The absence of the heat sent a chill throughout her, and it took a moment to gather her thoughts.

"We've got it designed so that it will be ideal for couples and growing families by taking down this wall." She pointed to the same one she'd shown Roman earlier in the week and continued pointing out the different elements throughout the homes. After several minutes, she sat back, watching Silvain's expression and body language.

The man rubbed the stubble on his chin, lifting a sheet of the plans and putting it back down as he continued to glance over the paperwork. Finally, he said, "I love it. Opening up the rooms, creating a better flow, your ideas for trans-forming current tenants' homes."

He stopped a moment, and when he spoke again, emotion was evident in his voice. He jabbed his finger into the plans as he looked between the two of them. "This is exactly what I wanted. Taking care of current and future clients is what I want as the legacy of the Guilbert family. Let's talk numbers."

The rest of the meeting passed a bit slower as Isabelle did her best to follow the conversation. At one point, she wished she could just leave, but she realized this was the best busi-ness training she would ever get.

As the negotiations tapered off for the day, Silvain talked proudly of his wife and children, boasting about several funny bits of his life. When he was done, the three of them stood, and he asked, "What is the nature of your relationship? I noticed a ring on her finger and am curious if you are engaged."

She could feel Roman tense next to her and saw his jaw drop open out of the corner of her eye. "We—"

"It happened a few nights ago," Isabelle said, taking a step back and slipping her arm through Roman's.

Silvain's face beamed. "I'm glad to hear it. I know you're not your father, but having a strong woman by your side helps me feel more at ease with the decision to hand over a property I've loved for more than forty years."

The man shook their hands and walked out of the restaurant.

The stiffness in Roman's body hadn't changed. If anything, it had gotten worse with the last comments from Silvain.

Turning to face him, Isabelle asked, "Are you all right?"

"Why did you do that?" His words were harsh and little more than a whisper. He wouldn't look at her.

"Do what? Say that we are engaged?"

When he nodded, she continued. "After all of his talk about family, I knew it was important to him."

He finally lifted his eyes to hers and glared at her, a flash of anger moving across them.

Isabelle took a step back, not sure what had happened. She didn't think it would be a big deal to tell a small white lie to the man. As little as they knew of each other, she wished they could at least begin a relationship.

"Is that what you do? Go around telling everyone you're engaged? Because there's no way you'd want to marry a guy who looks like me." He turned away and started walking out of the restaurant.

Isabelle ran to catch up, jumping in front of him so he'd have to stop. "What are you talking about? From everything I've learned about you, I'd be lucky to be your girlfriend or wife or whatever."

The word wife sent a flurry of excitement through her. She needed to calm down and figure out what his anger was about.

"Yeah right. Women haven't given me a second look since the accident." There were tears forming in his eyes, making the green irises look even more glassy.

Isabelle reached forward and took his hand, cutting the distance between them into just a few inches. "Well, then, it was their loss. I think your scar makes you look even more handsome than before."

The corners of Roman's mouth turned up. "How do you know what I looked like before? Did you look me up?"

Biting her bottom lip, Isabelle dipped her head and finally said, "Maybe."

"You're not just saying that to make me feel better, are you?"

Isabelle raised her head and saw his gaze flick to her lips. She wished he would lean forward and kiss her. She shook her head. "No, that was my first impression when I saw your old picture on the internet."

His gaze went to her lips again and lingered.

Isabelle held her breath as he slowly leaned forward. When her eyes started to go cross-eyed, she closed them, ready for the same electricity to pass through their lips that had flowed between their hands.

"Are you ready to go—oh, sorry." Sam's voice sounded apologetic, but Roman stepped back and looked at her again, conflicting emotions crossing his face. With the moment gone, he motioned for her to lead out and into the car.

As much as Isabelle tried to quiet her insides, she knew that even though they hadn't kissed, she was falling for Roman Hamilton.

CHAPTER 19

*R*oman sat a few inches from Isabelle, not sure if he should reach over with his hand and grab hers. He wanted to do it, but he also didn't want to fall for a girl who probably had suitors lined up for miles now that she was no longer engaged. What had her ex been like and would a relationship between Roman and Isabelle even work out?

"Are we heading to the restaurant, sir?" Sam asked from the driver's seat as they moved into the city.

"Yes, Sam. Our reservation is in a few minutes." He looked down at his phone to make sure he had the right time and then clicked it to black.

Isabelle turned to him. "Reservations already? I'm surprised you didn't ask me for a recommendation." She gave him a half-smile, and tingles shot through his body.

"I didn't make them, but I do travel here often, so I have a relatively good idea of where to go." He leaned over, drinking in her floral perfume, and whispered, "We're going to Le Meurice, by the way."

Her eyes went big, and her smile transformed her face from beautiful to downright stunning.

"I love that place. I've only been once, but it's food I dream of on a consistent basis."

Raising his eyebrow, Roman asked, "You dream of food?"

"You don't?" Isabelle chuckled. "I dream of my mother's homemade beef stew and ballet."

"Ballet?"

Nodding, she said, "I took ballet for quite a few years. It was something I loved more than a lot of things, but I injured my knee and couldn't turn out as far as before. I had to give it up when I was sixteen, and it was the hardest few months of my life, trying to figure out my identity after."

"Are there a lot of opportunities to continue it as a profession?" Roman felt out of his element talking about anything to do with dancing. His sisters were more into books and boys than any other extracurricular activities, and with them as his only reference point, he just wanted her to keep talking to him about it.

She smiled. "Not a ton, and it's ruthless from what I've heard. I've always thought it would be fun to dance with the Royal Ballet. But those are dreams of the past. I need to start planning things I want to accomplish now that I'm a soon-to-be business owner. I filed all the paperwork before we flew here, so I hope I didn't miss anything."

"Congrats on that!"

"What is it you've always wanted to do?" she asked, her eyes closer now as she leaned in, allowing him to see the dark blue around the rim and the middle a few shades lighter.

He shook his head to remember what she'd asked him. "Write books. But that's something for the future."

Sam stopped the car and walked around to open the door. Roman stepped out and turned to help Isabelle, and they moved into the restaurant.

Walking up to the hostess, he said, "We're here with another couple. It should be under Delacroix."

Isabelle grabbed his arm and pulled him to look at her, her face a mixture of excitement and confusion. "We're eating with my sister?"

He nodded and slipped his hand in hers before following the waitress back to the table.

Juliette and Tristan were sitting side by side, looking over their menus. Tristan looked up first and, seeing them, bumped Juliette with his elbow. She stood and came around the table, wrapping her sister in a hug.

Isabelle dropped Roman's hand to hug her sister, and he felt strange without the contact. Tristan walked up and shook hands before they pulled each other in for a half-hug. They all took their seats, and Roman could tell Juliette was eyeing him. He tugged at his collar, feeling exposed and under a microscope.

"What a surprise! Roman didn't tell me we were going to meet up with the two of you." Isabelle's words came out so fast he was sure a few French words filtered in, her accent more pronounced around her sister.

Juliette grinned. "He texted Tristan earlier that you'd figured out all the connections. What a small world."

"Small is the right word for it," Roman said, chuckling. What were the odds that he'd be falling in love with the sister of Tristan's girlfriend? That wasn't a bad thing, though, because then they could do stuff together and not be annoyed by one of the people in the other couple.

Taking a sip of her drink, Juliette turned her gaze back to Roman. "So, you saved my sister from working for Darcy Stewart? I don't know how I can repay you for that, but it was time."

Roman nodded. "She has an eye for design, and I think it

will work out better for her to be her own boss than to waste good talent on running errands."

Isabelle clasped her hands together. "I submitted all the papers to create a business before we came here."

Juliette reached out and touched Isabelle's hand. "I'm so glad. What are you naming your business?"

"Belle Rousseau Staging and Design. I wanted it to mean something and always push me when I see it."

"That works well, sis." Juliette let out a light squeal, and Isabelle giggled. "I just didn't think you'd ever leave Darcy."

Roman felt Isabelle tense up a bit, and thinking back to her reaction to his tension during the meeting earlier, he slid his hand over and took hers in it, squeezing lightly to let her know he was there.

"It was scary. I didn't want to be known as the failure of the family." Isabelle's words had a bite to them, and Roman silently cheered her on.

Juliette's eyes went wide. "I didn't mean it to be a bad thing, Isa. I know how hard it is to start your own company and be worried about it working out, but it sounds like you've got a great start already." She teared up a bit. "I'm so happy for you."

Isabelle reached up and wiped a tear away, and Roman turned to Tristan, hoping he'd have some guidance for dealing with the situation. Shrugging, Tristan looked down at the menu again, and Roman took that as his cue to let the sisters have a moment to themselves.

The next two hours passed with them enjoying their entrees and then dessert, talking and laughing at just about everything. It was something Roman enjoyed so much that he wished he and Isabelle were actually a couple. Had her words earlier been real? Did he have a chance with her?

After only knowing each other for two weeks, he knew he needed to just relax and not worry about it so much. He still had a lot of responsibilities, and if a relationship were to work out, she'd need to know his time would be divided. Pushing the thoughts away, he held the door for the others as they all filed out of the restaurant.

The sisters hugged, and Tristan smiled at Roman. "Looks like you're taking my advice."

Roman frowned. "Advice about what?"

"Finding a girl. She's a good one."

Shaking his head, Roman said, "We're not dating. She's helping me get this property, and I'm helping her with work since she just started."

"Uh-huh. Whatever you need to tell yourself, buddy. I see the way you look at her. Like a puppy dog."

Roman thrust out his elbow, jabbing Tristan in the side. That brought the girls' attention back to them, and both men pointed at one another as if trying to get out of some punishment.

"It was good to see you, T. I'll be back in a couple of weeks, but you're allowed to come to London and actually work on my marketing." Roman laughed.

"Please. I'm always working on your marketing. I had to hire someone else to take over your social media accounts because of how many comments you get."

They shook hands, and Roman said, "I've got to head out to see Evan in Vegas next week. Is there anything you need me to take to him?"

Tristan bunched up his fist. "This." He pretended to slug Roman, and Isabelle squeaked, making them all laugh. "Tell him to get us the details for the IBC reunion. My schedule fills up quickly, and it's his turn to plan it."

"Will do."

Sam pulled up with the car, and they said goodbye to Juliette and Tristan.

"Where to?" Sam asked.

Looking at the clock on the dash, Roman saw it was eight o'clock; he wasn't ready to head back to the hotel. Turning to Isabelle, he said, "What do you think? Are you up for giving me that native tour of Paris now?"

"Of course."

CHAPTER 20

*S*am had dropped them off in the middle of town, and they'd been walking around, enjoying the beautiful August evening. A lot of people rushed about, but Isabelle was determined to share the highlights of the city with Roman.

They saw the Eiffel Tower from a distance, and she led him away from it. After some time, they started to climb a slight hill where dozens of steps awaited them at the top.

"I didn't realize I'd be getting in a workout on this tour," Roman said with a grin.

"You'll survive. Besides, you'll get a real taste of Paris up there."

By the time they made it to the top step, Isabelle's breathing was slightly labored, but Roman bent over, looking as though he was trying to draw in every bit of air possible.

She looked up, and the brightness of the lights around the building caused the whiteness of the structure to be almost blinding at first. Roman stood next to her, and she looked up at his face, smiling as she saw the wonder in his eyes.

"This is amazing. I think I've seen it from far away, but this is incredible. What's it called again?"

"The Sacré-Cœur. It means 'sacred heart.' It's one of my favorite places because," she paused, helping him turn around, "it has one of the best views of the city."

He sat down on the stair and stared out at the lights below. Isabelle dropped down beside him, the sight below them making her fall in love with the spot all over again. When he turned to look at her, she realized how close they were, seeing a few light flecks of yellow in his emerald green eyes.

"What is it about this spot that you love so much?" His grin turned sly, and Isabelle groaned inwardly. She should have known he would ask such a thing.

She turned her gaze forward for a time, hoping to give herself a moment to think. This had been one of those things her family had always made fun of her for.

Without looking at him, she said, "Many tourists think it's romantic to go to the Eiffel Tower, but there's something about this place that draws me in. The beauty of the building and the landscape below is amazing. But the best part is what's just back here." She stood, motioning to a narrow path on the side of the building.

She reached out her hand, and he placed his in hers as he stood, covering hers almost completely. With his touch and his presence in this place, the place she'd dreamed of some romantic moment between her and a guy she was in love with seemed like it was actually coming to pass. Looking at him, she realized more than ever how much she'd fallen for this man before her, but did he feel the same?

After they wove through some alleys, they arrived in a small courtyard. A French tune was being played either live or streaming through the speakers, and several tables sat against the buildings, occupied by couples out for a night together.

Roman smiled, a deep chuckle erupting up his throat. "This is amazing. It's just the way some of the movies portray Paris, the way it was thirty years ago."

Isabelle reached out and pulled him toward one of the few empty tables. "Let's sit for a bit." A waitress came by, taking their drink order and then hurrying away.

Leaning forward on the table on her elbows, Isabelle rested her head on her hands, enjoying the look of awe on Roman's face. "You'd think it was Christmas morning, the way you're looking at this place."

He turned to look at her, his smile just as wide. "I never expected it to look like this here. It makes me wonder what I've missed in all the places I've traveled to."

"Maybe if you schedule some time to look around, you'd be able to find these kinds of things." Isabelle tried to hide her smile, but it broke through anyway.

Roman grinned. "You're probably right about that."

They talked about little things for the next hour, laughing and drinking their sodas. She led the way back through the path and was surprised when Roman's hand caught hers, their fingers intertwining. She didn't look at him, sure she would do something ridiculous and ruin the moment.

Once they made it to the front of Sacré-Cœur, Roman tugged on her hand before they descended the steps, pulling her up short.

"Did you forget something at the table?" she looked up and asked him.

He stepped forward, his presence causing the breath to catch in her throat. Letting go of her hand, he raised his hands and cupped the sides of her face.

His voice came out soft and deep, sending a chill throughout her body. "I did forget one thing." He moved forward, his lips brushing against hers, and then pulled her closer.

Her legs were weak, and as she deepened the kiss, some part of her subconscious recognized that this was it, what she'd dreamed of for so long.

As he pulled back, her lips felt like they were on fire. Reaching up, she touched them with her fingers. She saw him watching her, and they both started laughing at once.

He reached forward and took her hand in his again, descending the stairs at a casual pace. They didn't say anything, and Isabelle knew she'd never forget the magic of this moment.

CHAPTER 21

*D*uring negotiations the following day, Isabelle and Roman had no trouble pretending to be engaged. Isabelle made sure not to be a complete sap, but every time she looked at Roman, she felt her stomach flip and the butterflies take off. She loved the feel of her hand in his, and when he put his arm around her shoulders and pulled her to him, she fit perfectly beneath his arm and against his chest.

"Will you join us this evening?" Silvain asked as they finished the negotiations. "My family would like to meet you, and my wife has prepared a meal for all of us."

Roman turned to Isabelle, his eyes searching her face for the answer.

She smiled and nodded.

With that, Roman turned and said, "We can delay our trip home a bit longer. What time should we meet?"

"I'll tell her to have it ready earlier so you can fly out this evening if need be. How does six o'clock sound?"

"We can do that," Roman said. "Thank you, sir."

Isabelle glanced down at her watch as they left the building, seeing they still had several hours to go.

Roman must have seen the look because he said, "What do you want to do for the next four hours?"

Laughing, Isabelle tried to think about that as he wrapped one arm around her waist on the way out to the car. It relaxed her even more than before, and she wondered how she could have ever liked Aaron since he never gave any of those small touches and warm looks.

"How about a siesta?" she suggested as they got in the car.

"A what?"

"A siesta. It means nap in Spanish."

Roman's eyes went wide. "You know Spanish too?"

Isabelle threw back her head and chuckled. "No, just a few words here and there. You have to know what the word is for nap." She grinned at him, and he returned the expression.

"Well, I could use a nap for sure. Maybe a shower to prepare myself for meeting all these people tonight. I think Silvain's family is pretty big. How did you guess that he'd want us to meet his family before we left London?" He gave her a crazed expression, and Isabelle couldn't help but laugh.

"From everything you've told me about him, he seems like a family man, and with how he wanted to keep things for his tenants, I could imagine he'd want to introduce you to them." Remembering his stiff posture during the meeting with Silvain the day before, she asked, "Why were you so tense yesterday? During the meeting, you looked like you had a board tied to your back."

His jaw shifted back and forth, and he finally looked at her, a vulnerability in his eyes. "Mr. Guilbert is one of the victims of my father's schemes. I just hate it when people see me for my scar or for being Peter Hamilton's son, thinking I'll do the same thing as my father. Silvain has been very gracious at looking past all that, but it's still hard because I don't want to screw up the newfound trust."

His words seemed to stir something inside her, and she knew she could relate, at least on some level.

"Was it hard? Trying to work through a business your father had almost destroyed?" She tried to keep her expression neutral, knowing this was something difficult for him.

He flashed her a grim smile as he nodded. "More than I wanted to admit at the time. It was difficult getting people to work with us, at least on the larger homes. That's why I started doing real estate developing. I invested almost everything I had into this one property just outside London and sold the homes one by one. By year three, things were a lot better, but every once in a while, I meet someone my father betrayed, and it's hard to not feel two inches tall."

Isabelle didn't have the words to comfort him, so she leaned against his shoulder, slipping her hand into his and intertwining their fingers. She wouldn't worry about the status of their relationship just yet. She didn't want to crash with the reality that she probably didn't deserve a man such as Roman.

Back in the hotel room, Roman lay down on the bed, closing his eyes as memories of the day washed over him. He'd been pushing himself for so long that allowing a few moments like this seemed wasteful. But something inside him said he needed to slow down a bit and enjoy what was around him.

He enjoyed being around Isabelle. She'd gone through a lot in her life, even in the past several weeks, but what was so refreshing about her was that she wasn't afraid of his scar, and she wasn't afraid of the things he'd told her.

Reflecting back to the kiss the night before, a thrill ran up his spine. It had been his first kiss in years, at least since before the accident, and the softness of her lips and the sparks flying between them trumped every kiss he'd ever had before. It was like pure magic, and he hoped it wouldn't stop.

His phone rang, and Roman groaned, rolling over to see it on the nightstand. Tristan.

Swiping to pick it up, he said, "What's going on, T.?"

"Are you heading back to London already?"

"No, Mr. Guilbert invited us for a family dinner. After

everything my father did to hurt his family, it's a small peace offering to attend. I just hope they don't want to eat me alive for being related to the man."

Tristan chuckled. "Good luck with that. I wanted to ask you more about how things are really going between you and Isabelle. I'm assuming she is the girl you told me about last week."

The fact that it wasn't a question made Roman smile. That was Tristan's calling card, to state things he noticed and silently demand an answer.

"Yeah, I really like her, T. She's upbeat and fun, and she has such a great eye for what she does. Besides that, she's not scared of my appearance."

"Please, I don't know why you're still playing that card all the time. The scar didn't change your appearance that much. Juliette even said you're good-looking."

Roman laughed. "Are you worried I'm going after your girlfriend, T.?"

"Nope. I just want to make sure you're thinking straight. Just remember her fiancé broke up with her a couple of weeks ago. I just don't want you to get too far in and then have her realize she changed her mind or something like that."

The words burned in Roman's chest as if he'd been branded. "I'll be fine. I'm taking things slow—"

"How slow? Have you kissed her?"

When Roman didn't respond, Tristan said, "If this is slow for you, I wonder what fast would look like."

"I'll be careful. We just got caught up in the moment. We were walking around Sacré-Cœur, and it just felt right."

"Ahhh, that place is near magical. Well, I've got to run and meet Juliette, but just know I'm here if you need to talk about any relationship stuff. I've just been through all that, so I'm practically an expert."

Shaking his head, Roman said, "You wish."

They said their goodbyes, and Roman stared at the ceiling, pondering over Tristan's words. Had he been reading Isabelle all wrong? She seemed interested in him, and she definitely hadn't pulled away when he'd kissed her the night before.

He just needed his feelings to turn down to a simmer and take his time with whatever was going on. As much as he wanted to be in a relationship all of a sudden, he wasn't ready for any kind of heartbreak.

CHAPTER 23

A knock sounded on the door an hour later, and when Roman answered it, he couldn't help but smile at Isabelle practically bouncing on her toes as she grinned at him.

"Are you ready to go?"

Roman looked back at the clock on the nightstand. "We still have an hour and a half before we have to be there. What are you so excited for?"

"I have an idea, but we need to go now to get it done so we can still be on time to the party."

Trying to decide if he trusted her as Tristan's words ran through his mind, he shrugged and walked over to the bathroom to throw on a new shirt and pull on his dress shoes. Taking his phone and his wallet, he walked back to the door. "Okay, where are we headed?"

He watched her bite her bottom lip as they walked to the elevator. "It's a surprise?" The words sounded more like a question, causing a small pit to form in his stomach. He wished he hadn't picked up Tristan's call because now he was going to overanalyze every detail of his time with Isabelle. Apparently, it wasn't only girls who did that.

Walking out to the car, Sam gave him a worried look, as if already part of this master plan.

Roman helped Isabelle into the back seat before turning to Sam and asking softly through clenched teeth, "What does she have in mind for this surprise?"

"I'm not supposed to tell you yet, sir. I apologize, but you'll know in just a few minutes."

Frustration webbed through his chest, and Roman bit down hard, causing a jolting pain in one of his molars. Ducking down, he sat on the back seat, hoping he could make it through this. He'd never been one for surprises. All of the bad things in his life had always been prefaced as a surprise. Surprise, his father had been arrested. Surprise, his stepmother took off and left the kids with him.

His sisters weren't bad, and in many ways, helping to raise them had been a blessing in his life. Something to focus on when he didn't want to concentrate on how lonely he really was. The worst surprise of all had been the hit to his ego after the car accident. He could still see the whites of the driver's eyes as he turned too soon and T-boned Roman's car.

They drove a short distance down the road and pulled into a large open parking lot. Sam parked in the middle of it, and those knots tightened in his stomach again, as if sensing this surprise was going to be of the same caliber as the others.

Sam opened the door, and Roman and Isabelle got out. Roman glanced between the two of them, ready for the suspense to be over.

"What are we doing here?" he said with more gruffness than he'd intended.

He saw Isabelle's excitement falter somewhat, and he

tried to smile, even though his insides made him feel as if he would vomit at any moment.

"We are going to practice driving. Well, by 'we,' I mean you. I asked Sam to let you drive around this parking lot for a bit. Maybe it will help you get over some of the fears you have."

A sourness spread through his mouth, and he shook his head. "No. I'm lucky I can get into the back of a car. Driving? That's not going to happen."

Pursing her lips, Isabelle straightened, trying to match eyes with him even though she was several inches shorter. Waving her arms around, she said, "There are no other cars here right now. What better way to ease you back into this than by driving here? All you have to do is get behind the wheel and drive for just a few minutes."

"I can't do it."

Isabelle folded her arms, her eyebrows raised as she challenged him. "You mean won't do it. Do you really want to depend on Sam the rest of your life to get anywhere?" She turned to Sam and said, "You're a great driver. I don't mean to slight you. I just think he needs to get past this already."

To Roman's dismay, Sam nodded. "I agree."

"Traitor." Roman's whisper didn't have an effect on Sam's neutral expression, and he wished he could go back to his hotel room and just kip, just sleep his way past this whole situation. Tension built in his shoulders, and it felt as if he'd never be able to swallow the large mound that had formed in his throat.

Isabelle took the keys from Sam and gave them to Roman. "You can choose which one of us sits in the passenger seat."

He could tell he wasn't getting out of this, and as much as he wanted to sit down and tell them there was no way he would do it, he knew it was better than hearing her bug him for the next hour.

"Sam." He saw a flash of disappointment cross her face and said, "He's a great driver. And he didn't force me into this." His tone came out harsher than he'd intended, but with all of the emotions and alarms sounding in his head, that was the best he could do.

Isabelle grimaced, folding her arms across her chest. She bit her bottom lip and took a step back. It was odd to see her so quiet, so withdrawn, but he couldn't worry about that now.

Roman shook his head. "You need to use this pushiness to get contracts for your business. You're a lot better than you think you are at persuasion."

Her face fell, but he had a hard time finding compassion or feeling bad when this had all been her idea. What had she expected when she had no idea what he'd been dealing with all these years? All she knew was that he'd been in an accident.

Turning, he opened the driver's side door, feeling odd that it was on the opposite side from London. He'd driven in the States during college, but everything felt so foreign. With his seatbelt fastened, he stuck the key into the ignition and turned it on, sitting back and taking a breath before moving his hands to the wheel.

Sam slid in next to him with one corner of his mouth slightly raised. "Are you ready for this?"

"No. But I'm not in the mood to hear about it for the next five days."

He took another breath and moved the shifter down to drive, willing his foot to leave the brake. They coasted along for a few moments before he slammed it down again, throwing both of them forward with the jerk.

"You're fine, sir. Just keep going."

After fifteen minutes of coasting and going no more than fifteen miles per hour, Roman shifted the car into park beside Isabelle and looked out the window, feeling a little better. She was looking so forlorn that he felt pity for her. She wouldn't even look him in the eyes. Even though he didn't appreciate being forced into the situation, he realized she'd only been trying to help him. He didn't need to act like a jerk, especially when it was apparent she felt bad about it all. "Okay, Isabelle. It's your turn."

Sam left the car, and she slid into the passenger seat, still wearing a somber expression. Roman's frustration with her was nearly gone as he had gone further and faster than he had in five years.

"You're doing so well. We can stop if you need to. I'm sorry I pushed you into doing this at all. I guess I didn't realize how deep your fear went." Tears were forming in her eyes, and his irritation at her presumption softened a little more.

"Once more around the parking lot, and then we need to get to the dinner."

Roman shifted back into drive and decided to press the gas a bit more this time, hoping the lack of panic he'd had with Sam in the car was a sign that enough time had passed.

Isabelle reached over and squeezed his hand before turning back to look out the front window. Watching the speedometer raise from ten to fifteen and finally twenty, Roman blew out a long breath, feeling the excitement spread through him. He was actually driving.

Making it around one corner of the lot, he noticed something out of the corner of his eye. A car was coming in their direction, not driving too fast, but within seconds, the little yellow car turned into the little white one from his dreams, slamming into the side. Roman could feel the pain again, his arm broken and his leg pinned against the door.

Slamming on the brake, he threw the shifter into park and shoved the door open. Doubling over, he felt sweat break out on his forehead, and he was struggling to get air into his chest. A droplet of water rolled down his face, and he wasn't sure if it was from the sweat or the tears that had formed. He was still just as scared as ever, and he hoped he'd be able to make it long enough in the car to get to the Guilbert's home.

A hand rubbed at his back, and he turned to see a mixture of fright and guilt on Isabelle's face. Sniffling, she whispered, "I'm sorry, Roman. I didn't know it would still be this bad. I just thought—"

He stood, not ready to be comforted just yet. "Give me a minute." With his breathing coming out in rapid spurts, he walked around, doing every breathing exercise he could think of to calm down. At least this time there was no pain, physically anyway. It would take more time to get him behind the wheel of a car.

Sam stepped forward. "It's time, Mr. Hamilton. If we don't leave now, we'll be late."

Roman nodded and waved Isabelle to the car. He needed to refocus. Tonight would be about saying thank you for the property and giving an apology for his father's actions.

CHAPTER 24

*A*rriving at the Guilbert's home, Isabelle still felt guilty for forcing Roman to conquer his fears when she hadn't even conquered her own. His comment about using her persuasion for her business had about broken her heart. To some degree, it had been a compliment, but she also realized that her pushiness had been the cause for the trauma he'd relived earlier. She wanted the confidence that at least a few people believed in her ability to run a business, especially when she didn't quite believe in herself yet, but she wished his words had come under better circumstances. She was afraid she'd broken his trust in her.

As they exited the car and moved toward the front door of the large French home, Isabelle looked down at her feet, hoping she could be the support he needed for this evening. She looked up when he slipped his hand around hers, not glancing in her direction as they waited for the door to open.

A small brunette opened the door and said, "Oh, you must be Mr. Hamilton and Ms. Rousseau. Please come in. I'm Charlotte, Silvain's wife. I was just getting some things to take out back. You can go ahead and move through those glass doors and out into the backyard. There is quite the crowd out there, excited to meet you."

Roman's hand tightened around Isabelle's, and his jaw flexed as it worked back and forth.

Leaning closer to him, she whispered, "You can do this. Just be you and listen to them."

She knew that was easier said than done, especially after she'd just forced him to relive some of the hardest memories of his life.

Giving her a tight smile, he let go of her hand and waved her forward, opening the door. They walked out into the shadow of the house, and Isabelle noted that two large trees shaded much of the backyard, and in the August weather, that was a nice advantage. A couple of kids ran around, one of the girls chasing a boy a little bigger than she. Several adults sat around a few of the tables set out on the lawn, and the smell of food floated through the air toward Isabelle, reminding her it had been some time since she'd eaten.

"I'm glad you're here. We were getting worried you'd taken off back to London." Silvain's voice boomed, and several people turned in their direction.

Roman grinned, and his shoulders relaxed a touch. "No, sir. We wouldn't miss this dinner for the world."

Silvain beamed and motioned for them to follow him to a table occupied by several people. "These are the Bernard family. They live in one of the units we've been discussing today."

Roman nodded and smiled, Isabelle following suit.

Moving to another table, the older man introduced them to a few other families that already occupied the property Roman had just purchased. She liked watching Roman interact with them, assuring them they would like the new changes coming.

The last table was filled with two teenage girls, three teenage boys, and an older boy in his early twenties.

"These are my grandchildren. Their parents are over there cooking the food and helping Charlotte arrange everything. I hope you both brought an appetite."

As if by command, Isabelle's stomach growled, and her eyes widened. "Sorry."

"That means you are ready to eat. Come, sit at this table over here as my esteemed guests."

Roman pulled out the chair, allowing Isabelle to sit down before he pushed it in. He sat next to her, his leg bouncing under the table at least a mile a minute. She touched it with light pressure, and he turned to look at her, a questioning look on his face.

"Relax," she said in an undertone. "You're doing fine."

The food was delicious, making Isabelle homesick for her mother's cooking and their family get-togethers in Dinan.

Silvain stood after some time and said, "We are grateful for this new relationship we have with Magnolia Property Group and hope this agreement will last far into the future." He raised his glass, and the rest of the group toasted each other, wine glasses clinking around all of the tables.

A few moments later, Roman stood, surprising her. With one hand in his pocket and one holding on to his glass of soda, he said, "Thank you to the Guilbert family and anyone else who helped with that delicious meal. It was amazing." He paused a moment, and she could see he was trying to gather his thoughts.

"Standing before you is kind of a scary thing, and I don't get all that scared often. Well, except..." he looked down at Isabelle and gave her a cockeyed smile. "Anyway, I am honored to be working with such great people. My history isn't always the greatest when it comes to family, but your close-knit family and friends make me want a future like that."

"The two of you will have it if you want," Silvain shouted from his seat, sending a wave of laughter through the group.

For a moment, Roman looked as though he didn't understand, so Isabelle poked his leg, gesturing to the engagement ring on her finger. Recognition flashed over his face, and he smiled at the crowd.

Nodding, he said, "Absolutely. But I just want to stand here and publicly apologize to you all for what my father did in the past. I've done a lot of that over the years, but as Monsieur Guilbert told me the other day, it's what we do moving forward that will repair what happened in the past. I hope to make it up to you as this change goes forward." Raising his glass, he took a sip, and Isabelle did the same, tasting the tartness of the wine.

The party lasted until late into the night, and by the time they made it back to the hotel, Isabelle wasn't sure she would make it to the bed before falling asleep. All the emotions of the day caught up to her.

"Thank you, Isabelle," Roman's rich voice said as she used her key card to open her hotel room door.

"For making you relive old memories? I'm not sure you should be thanking me for that." She rolled her lips in, trying to look as apologetic as she felt.

Roman chuckled, but even the sound of it didn't make her feel better. "It was good to see that I've made some progress, but I still have a ways to go. Thank you for standing by me at the dinner tonight. It was difficult going, knowing these people suffered because of my father, but it felt right to apologize and hopefully move forward, proving that I will take care of them."

"It was really sweet what you did, and what you said to

them. I can only imagine how it's been to have your whole life changed by someone else's decisions."

Roman took a step back. "Be ready early. Sam wants to beat a storm in the forecast."

Isabelle waved a hand. "There's always a storm in the forecast when it comes to London."

"How right you are." Roman smiled, but it held no warmth.

"Roman, again, I'm really sorry about earlier. I should have realized it wouldn't be that simple for you to get over. I just wanted to help you the way you helped me."

He ran a hand through his hair and took a deep breath. Isabelle held her breath as she waited for his answer, hoping he'd trust her again, or at least know how sorry she really was.

"It's been five years since my accident, but I still have vivid dreams of that night. I can feel the pain when I see the accident in my mind. That's why I don't drive myself around. That's why I freaked out today." His words were flat, and Isabelle's heart went out to him.

"What can I do to make it up to you? I'll do whatever you need me to do to make it right." Isabelle could hear the hope in her voice, as well as pleading. She didn't want to destroy the best relationship she'd ever had because she didn't think about the consequences.

Pulling his key card out for the room next door, he flashed her a small smile and reached out to gently brush his thumb across her cheek. "I know you meant well. Just give me a little time. See you in the morning." He disappeared into his room, leaving Isabelle standing in the hallway. She felt as if she'd been punched in the gut. She'd made a bigger mistake than she'd realized.

CHAPTER 25

The next week passed, and Roman was surprised at how much delegating had helped him get things taken care of while he was gone. He remembered Dan Montgomery, his mentor in college, and all of the wisdom he'd shared over the years Roman had been at Hawthorne. One thing he remembered in particular now was that life passed whether you were working or not. There was a time to work and a time to play, so to speak. Since Roman had taken over Magnolia, he hadn't taken time to enjoy some of the things he loved most.

Tristan had assigned one of his employees to create a website and other social media platforms for Isabelle's business, allowing her to focus on the Paris property. She'd been in Paris since a few days after their negotiations, executing her plans on the former Guilbert property. As nervous as she'd been to take over something of that scale on her own, Roman knew she could do it. There was something deep inside her that just needed a little boost of confidence to reveal it.

It had taken several days for him to get past the driving

incident, and he was grateful she seemed remorseful about it. She'd apologized several times, and he'd finally told her not to worry about it, that he was over it.

She'd said she was trying to help him like he'd helped her, but he was curious how he'd helped her. The only thing he'd done was ask her to take a risk, and she ended up fired because of it. Of course, he had enough work to keep her busy for more than a lifetime, but he realized people reacted differently to things. Many people had scoffed that he had such a hard time with driving around town after the accident, but everything was so real, as if it were happening all over again.

They hadn't made anything official and hadn't even talked about what their relationship meant, but he'd seen her without her engagement ring the day before and wondered what that meant for her. Had she completely gotten over her ex-fiancé? Would she even want a real relationship with Roman? He still wasn't sure about his feelings, but maybe dating was just another thing he had to conquer on his way to getting over the accident. He did know he was ready to hopefully delegate more and more of his business to allow him the time to enjoy life.

Roman texted Isabelle as he rode to the airport to catch his flight to Vegas. He would meet Evan there to find another resort property.

I'm heading to the airport now. I'll be away from my phone for a bit, so contact Shirley if there is anything you need. I'll call when I land. He pressed send and reread the words again.

A few minutes later, a text came in from her, causing him to smile.

Good luck! I hope you get there safe, and I'll wait for your call.

A shot of excitement ran through his chest. He liked the idea of having someone think about him while he traveled. His twin sisters didn't usually care, only calling him when he'd cut off their money supply. As much as Shirley cared about him and his schedule, she had a life and her own family to worry about.

Sam drove to the airport where Roman's private jet was housed. Once they parked the limo, he helped Roman with his bags as he moved up the ramp and into the cabin. International flights weren't always his favorite, as they took a lot of time and he felt jet-lagged for days, but he'd put off helping Evan for long enough. This trip needed to happen to help Evan find his next resort property.

Several hours and time changes later, Sam and Roman touched down in Las Vegas, bleary-eyed and ready for a shower. He'd forgotten to have Shirley make a car reservation for him and had pulled up a rental car website on his phone.

Sam said, "Sir, I think Mr. Pearson has sent a car." He pointed out the door, and Roman moved to see a black stretch limo waiting on the tarmac.

"Evan just won the good-friend award. I didn't feel like waiting for a car availability."

"Me either." Sam's smirk made Roman laugh. The man seemed to be loosening up at the rate of a moving snail, but it was progress nonetheless.

The man opened the door for them, and even though he couldn't see out the front window, Roman was amazed at the precision it took to navigate rush-hour traffic in a car so long. Dropping them off at one of Evan's current resorts, Roman felt a bit sick to his stomach and was grateful he didn't have to do any major thinking until the next day.

By the time they'd checked into their rooms, Roman had to rush to throw up in the bathroom. Feeling his forehead, he knew it was hotter than normal, but he didn't have the energy to do anything about it. Crawling into bed, he passed out without even having to turn on the telly to put him to sleep.

* * *

Isabelle tried to tell herself that everything was okay when twenty-four hours went by without a phone call or text from Roman. She'd already texted him twice but refrained from contacting Sam, even though she wanted to know what had happened. That's when all of the dark thoughts and fantasies started playing in her mind, and she hoped they hadn't come true, that the airplane had malfunctioned over a range of mountains or at sea.

She now knew that forcing him to drive had been a cruel joke, and she'd worried about it until he finally told her he was over it. Their relationship, such as it was, had been fragile since, but she'd found hope that he'd texted her before he'd left for the States. Now that he wasn't answering, she worried he wouldn't be around to see how his Paris project had turned out. Or see her again.

When another two days rolled past without word from him, she called Juliette.

"Hey, sis. What are you up to? Do you want to get lunch today?"

Isabelle closed her eyes. "I'll see what I have left to get done before the painters get here. Hey, do you know if Tristan has heard from Roman in the past couple of days?"

"Hmm…I'm not sure. I think he might have been texting him last night about something new his company has been working on for him, but I'm not sure."

Isabelle could hear her sister take a drink of something before she said, "Why? Has he not contacted you?"

"He said he'd call me when he landed, but that was two days ago, and I haven't heard from him."

"He's with Evan, so that could be the reason."

Isabelle frowned. "What's that supposed to mean?"

Juliette let out a quick laugh. "Evan is like the ultimate playboy of that group of guys. Out of the ten in the IBC, he lives in Vegas right now and owns resorts. You do the math."

Ignoring the prickle of jealousy creeping into her stomach, she said, "What's IBC?"

"Roman hasn't told you about it? It stands for International Billionaire Club. Ten of the guys from their frat house are now billionaires, so they meet once a year to reminisce and talk about business."

He and Tristan weren't the only ones who were billionaires so young? She'd just started feeling like things were getting better between her and Roman, but he was even more out of her league than Aaron had been. If only she could go back and redo the hour before the Guilbert's party, she would do it in a heartbeat.

"Do you ever worry about not being in the same social group as Tristan is?" Isabelle bit one of her fingernails, hoping to calm some of the jealous nerves mixing inside.

"Every once in a while. But he's been so good to me that I don't worry as much now."

Looking at the time, Isabelle said, "I should probably get back to the site. But will you have Tristan let me know if he hears from Roman at all? I'll try him again, but I have a few questions about keeping this project rolling."

"I'm sure you do." The teasing in Juliette's voice made her grit her teeth.

Hanging up, Isabelle paced a bit more in the small trailer they'd parked there for her office. She'd just have to brush it off. If going to Vegas and hanging out with Evan was going to make Roman forget all about her, she'd do the same to him.

She was a strong woman, and now that she'd been able to

get her business underway, she could make it. No matter what their relationship turned out to be, she would be grateful for the push and encouragement Roman had given her along the way.

Looking back at the sketches, she pulled up the list of phones numbers she still needed to call and got to work.

CHAPTER 26

"Hey, Isabelle. I'm sorry I haven't contacted you since I left London. I got really sick right after we got off the plane, and then we were constantly going as we toured a bunch of options for Evan. I've thought about you often, and I hope you're well. I'm heading to the airport now and will probably be back tomorrow night sometime. I haven't done the time change calculations, though. Just, well, call me."

Roman clicked the end button, hoping he didn't sound lame on the phone. After having the flu for several days and not enough time to recover, his body still ached. At least he was able to eat food now.

What had originally been slated as a week trip had turned into twelve days, but Roman was grateful to have helped Evan find another fixer-upper property he could turn into a resort. The one they'd stayed in was bigger than Roman remembered from when he'd helped his frat brother find it a few years before.

The flight seemed to drag on, and Roman didn't get much sleep, feeling like he'd been wrung out. He wasn't used to feeling like that, and he wondered if it was just another side effect of his body not completely healing from the illness and trying to do too much. What he wouldn't give to have Isabelle there right then. He just needed someone to tell him he'd be okay, even though right now he didn't feel like it.

He went through the voicemails and texts Isabelle had left once again, surprised to see how much she'd worried about him. As expected, he hadn't heard from the twins since he'd left, making his thoughts lean more toward the French woman who cared. With the twins about to start their own lives, he'd be alone soon, and no one would be worried about him. The thought warmed his heart even more to Isabelle's concerns.

Once they arrived, Sam pulled the car around, and Roman was grateful for it, sliding into the comfortable and the familiar, falling asleep again on the ride home.

"Sir, we've arrived at your home."

Roman woke up to find Sam shaking him, a groggy sleep making his body feel heavy and like he couldn't get it to obey the commands coming from his brain.

Finally moving his feet out of the car, he made his way to the front door and walked in.

Beth saw him and said, "What happened to you?"

Faking a grin, Roman said, "It's nice to see you too. I've been sick. Has Mrs. Ashton been here often?"

Heels clicked along the hardwood floor, and Roman slipped onto a stool next to the long island, not sure if he'd be able to support himself completely if he stood much longer.

"I'm still here, Mr. Hamilton. We had no incidents while you were away. The girls have been a joy to be with." The woman smiled at him, as if the accomplishment of staying with two eighteen-year-old girls and keeping them alive was worthy of a medal.

"How much did they pay you to say all that?" he asked with a smirk.

He felt a jab in the side and turned to find Anne frowning at him. "We've missed out on a lot because of your long trip. Mrs. Ashton wouldn't let us go anywhere."

Beth placed her hands on her hips. "We go to university next week, and then we won't be babysat like we're in primary school again."

Roman dug into his wallet and took out several fifty-pound notes, laying them in the open palm Mrs. Ashton held out. Her eyes grew wider, and he added another two just for good measure.

"Thank you, Mrs. Ashton, for staying with the girls. I really appreciate it. I know they can be a handful."

The woman nodded, and Roman rose, doing his best to will his legs to escort her to the door.

She turned around just as she reached it. "It really was no problem, Mr. Hamilton. Please, call me any time you need someone to help out."

She must have missed the part where the girls were leaving next week.

After seeing her out, Roman moved to his recliner, leaning it all the way back as he pulled a blanket over him. Taking out his phone, he dialed Isabelle. The call rang several times before going to her voicemail.

"Isabelle, just checking in. I made it home. I'm heading to bed, so I hope to talk to you in the morning. I hope...I hope you're doing well. I'll call again tomorrow."

He moved to his bed, feeling like he'd been hit by a ton of bricks with the weight of exhaustion filling him. He'd never felt like that before and wondered if it was a one-time thing or if he needed to slow down a lot more.

His last thoughts before drifting off to sleep were of Isabelle. He hoped she'd forgive him for the late contact and would give him a chance to explain. Now that he was on the offending side, it made him realize he should've forgiven her sooner for the car incident, especially when she was so sincere. If they were going to have a relationship, they'd have to be willing to have patience with one another. They had a lot to work through between the two of them, but she'd cared about him for who he was on the inside. She'd never flinched from him and his scar, never treated him differently because of it. She was someone he could keep around and build a life with forever.

* * *

ISABELLE SAW Roman's phone call the first time and missed it the second time. She wanted to be angry with him, wanted to yell and scream that she liked him and he obviously didn't feel the same. But after listening to his message, she knew his illness must have been the reason he hadn't checked in once he got there. That still didn't help, knowing that he'd contacted Tristan, though.

Since when did she become such a drama lover? She needed to relax and be patient. It sounded like Roman had been through a lot over his lifetime, and maybe that caused him to hold back a bit. Who was she kidding? A billionaire falling in love with her? It just brought back all the bad memories of Aaron.

The next morning, she made sure the new carpets were installed in the Paris units, as well as the appliances. The shiny stainless steel made the kitchens look sleek and high end but not so modern that real people wouldn't want to live there.

Several boxes she'd ordered had arrived, and she unpackaged a few of them in one unit, taking out the knobs for the drawers and cabinets. Locks for the doors had already been installed in all of them, but these were going to take a while. She was grateful she had a screwdriver as she got to work installing the small knobs throughout the first unit.

Her phone rang around eight in the morning, and she looked down. Roman's name on the screen sent a flood of emotions mixing in her stomach, and she wasn't quite sure what to do.

Swiping the screen, she did her best to keep her voice neutral. "Hello."

"Good morning. Ah, it's so good to hear your voice again. I'm so sorry I didn't call you when I got to Vegas."

Isabelle could tell he was sincere, but a part of her wasn't ready to let it slide just yet. "I got your message. I'm sorry you were sick."

"Thank you. I'm feeling better now, just knackered. I was—"

"Knackered?" Isabelle racked her brain trying to find a definition.

"Tired, exhausted, shattered." He paused a moment and Isabelle made a sound to make him know she was still there. "I was in bed for the first four days, and then we were going from morning to night, trying to find properties and negotiate to make up for that time. At least we found him something." He paused a moment, and when he spoke, his tone sounded hopeful. "Are you in Paris?"

"Yes. I'm just installing the handles and knobs I ordered. It will take me a while to get them all put on throughout the units, but I just put one on, and it looks really good." She was sitting on the floor and leaned back onto her hands, admiring the oil-rubbed bronze knob.

"Do you need some help?" he asked, his breathing heavier than normal.

The front door opened, and the footsteps on the front

entry made Isabelle panic a bit as she wasn't expecting any of the workers to be in this unit for the day.

Looking up, she saw Roman's smiling face, sending her stomach into its usual flip and butterflies scattering to different parts of her body. Traitorous body. She wanted to be mad at him for a few more days.

"What are you doing here? I thought you were in London."

"Sam flew me here this morning. I wanted to check on the project…and you."

Isabelle broke her gaze from his as he said the words, trying to process it all. She'd gone through every emotion, trying to reconcile why she felt so much for him and then hadn't heard from him in so long.

Roman sat a few feet from her. "You seem off. Did I interrupt something?" He looked around as if someone else was going to walk around the corner.

"No, I'm just bugged I didn't hear anything from you. I was worried. I kept having visions that you were sinking to a watery grave. When people care about each other, they contact one another." Her hands started moving, emphasizing her words, and it only added to the adrenaline moving through her, adding to her frustration. "You got mad about me wanting you to drive, which I now know was a big mistake, but not even sending me a text? Was that some kind of test? You had time to contact Tristen."

Roman looked as though he'd been slapped. Even the color of his scar had turned a faint pink instead of the usual bright color. "You're right. I'm sorry. I only contacted Tristen for work a couple of times. I'm not used to having people care where I am or if I'm safe. I'll know for next time. I'm way out of practice with this relationship stuff. I did love that you were concerned about me, for what it's worth." One corner of his mouth turned up, his face filled with hope.

She took in a breath and let it out slowly. At least there would be a next time. "I can't have a relationship without communication. If there is any hope for us, we'll have to work on that."

His shoulders relaxed as he grinned. "Deal."

Leaning over, she grabbed a screwdriver and handed it up to him.

He grinned. "What's this for?"

"You offered to help. And by myself, all of the hardware will take me until next week to get done." She smiled up at him and opened a new package, ready to put in the knob.

They worked methodically, chatting here and there about basic subjects. After a few hours, Isabelle's stomach growled, reminding her she needed to eat.

"Should we stop for some food?" Roman asked. "It sounds like your stomach is rioting."

They both laughed at that, and Isabelle liked the sound of his laugh.

"That might be a good idea."

They'd finished the hardware in the kitchen and had moved to the bathrooms an hour before. Standing up on the tile, she leaned over and reached her hand out.

Roman looked at it for a moment and then grabbed it with his own, almost pulling Isabelle down as he stood.

He grinned at her. "You're pretty strong."

Placing her hands on her hips, she said, "Does that surprise you?"

Laughter played on his lips, and he finally said, "No."

Their eyes locked, and Isabelle wondered what he was thinking. She wasn't even sure she knew what she was feeling at the moment.

The moment was broken as a text came in on his phone. He looked at it, and his fingers flew as he typed something in.

Putting it away again, he looked at her. The space between his eyebrows had creased.

"Is there something wrong?"

He shrugged. "Shirley just said there was a problem with one of our accounts. But I'm sure it's nothing. Let's get some food."

CHAPTER 27

Roman's time with Isabelle had been near perfect. They'd spent two days putting all the hardware in and talking about little things here and there, sometimes delving deeper into their pasts. Later on the second day, he finally asked her about her relationship with her ex-fiancé.

"What happened between you two?"

Isabelle looked at him, her expression neutral but the look in her eyes a little sad. When she spoke, she didn't look at him, concentrating on her hands.

"We met at university and had been dating the past few years. I always thought how lucky I was that I'd found someone like him. He had big goals and aspirations, and at first, I thought he made me a better person. I just didn't realize how blind I was to a lot of things."

Roman collected the plastic wrappers and took them over to a box they were using for rubbish. He didn't say anything, not wanting to press too much, even though his curiosity was through the roof right then.

"I'd met his family once or twice in the three years we'd been dating, but after we got engaged, he took me over for a family dinner. Walking into their large home, I felt as though I'd just stepped into a refrigerator. His mother ignored me as much as possible and kept bringing up this other girl's name, someone Aaron had gone to school with. I tried to shake it off, thinking I was overreacting."

Stuffing his hands into his pockets, Roman watched as she wrapped her arms around herself and studied the floor. The urge to comfort her was outweighed by wanting to hear the whole story, to understand what her hesitation was and to know if Tristan's words about her needing time were correct.

"What happened?"

She looked up at him then. "A couple of days later, we were heading to dinner when he had the driver stop the car. He turned and told me he didn't think this would work out, that I wouldn't help him reach his business and political goals because of my lack of knowledge in the business world." She sniffled and wiped at her nose with her hand. "He also said that design was a waste of time."

Roman watched her struggle to swallow and closed the distance between them, wrapping his arms around her. She didn't struggle, just leaned into him as the tears soaked into his t-shirt.

He rubbed his hand up and down her back. "Shhh. It's okay. It sounds like you dodged a bullet."

Her head lifted back, her eyes searching his. "What do you mean?"

"I mean that if he broke up with you because of all that—the encounter with his mother and not believing in what you are passionate about—you have the opportunity to make it so much better, and you can do what you love. Can you imagine being stuck in a relationship where you were just supposed to be the trophy wife on his arm? I can't see you liking something like that, even though you are one of the most beautiful women I've ever seen." He reached up, wiping away a tear that had slid down her cheek and then another that had just escaped.

He expected her to laugh about that, seeing her mind turning as her eyes darted around his face. "You're right." It sounded more like a revelation than anything. "I would have struggled with it."

Pausing before he asked the question he needed to know, he said, "You don't still love him?"

She pursed her lips and after a few moments finally said, "I don't think so. I think I just figured that was what my future looked like, that I was supposed to be with him. Now that I've had some time away, a new perspective, I think you're right. It worked out the right way."

"I see you aren't wearing the ring." He let one side of his mouth turn up, trying to get her to answer the question but making it more casual.

Isabelle looked down at her hand. "I took it off so I wouldn't ruin it with all of the work around here. But when I see the Guilberts, I have to wear it. Charlotte will make a big fuss about us having a fight or something."

Roman shifted a bit closer, knowing they had made a mess of the whole situation with the Guilberts, but something inside him made him want to give her his own ring, just so it wasn't a constant reminder of her ex.

She stepped out of his arms. "We should probably get this all cleaned up. I think we're done for now as far as my work is concerned. I'll return to put in the fixtures when they arrive, and then your clients can start moving in."

"You've done a great job with these." He grinned and pulled out his phone. "I'll get Sam to fly us back. Do you want to leave tonight or tomorrow?"

It was only five in the evening, and the quick flight wouldn't be awful. He wouldn't mind sleeping in his own bed again. As nice as the hotel's bed was, he hadn't been able to get the sleep he needed while he was in Vegas.

"How about tonight? It will be nice to be back in London."

He flashed her a mischievous grin. "The French girl feeling at home in London. I like it."

She giggled. "There's something about your own bed after a long day that seems really tempting."

After grabbing their things, Sam drove them back to the hotel, where they collected their things and headed for the small airport. Roman enjoyed Isabelle sitting next to him and realized how much he wanted this to be his reality, to have someone by his side to fly around the world and be there for him, just as the twins were about to abandon him to some degree, heading out on their own adventures. His home in London was going to feel even emptier without them around.

What he wanted was Isabelle, the girl who didn't shy away because of his scar and who didn't try to impress him because he had money. She was down to earth and beautiful, had great skills as a designer, and was easy to talk to, something he found as a rarity in most women. He just needed to find a way to tell her all that without scaring her. Should he wait days? Weeks? Time would tell.

CHAPTER 28

*A*fter a few days back in London, Roman settled back into a routine. There was so much to catch up on after nearly two weeks out of the office, but he was grateful for his employees who kept things rolling while he was gone.

Shirley came to him one morning, a worried expression on her face. "One of the accountants brought this to me this morning, sir. It's about that account I called you about while you were in Paris. I think there is something wrong with it."

"A client account or our bank account?" he asked, taking the paper from her hand.

"Bank. It looks like someone has gotten ahold of one of our cards and is spending large amounts on the internet."

Looking at the sheet, he found the card number and recognized it as being close to his own. "I gave my card to Isabelle. She's probably been using it to buy all the supplies."

Shirley frowned and shook her head. "I had one sent to her before she left for Paris, Mr. Hamilton. All of the purchases on that card add up, going to normal vendors. This card is yours, but it's been used for things like furniture and décor items."

"You can tell all that from this statement?" Roman could feel the unease and irritation take root in his chest.

Shaking her head, Shirley said, "No. I had the companies send me an itemized list of what was ordered, just to make sure it wasn't something needed for the units in Paris." She paused, looking as though she were trying to choose her words carefully.

"What's on your mind, Shirley?" Roman sat back, not sure he really wanted to know the woman's suspicions. They were probably the same as what he'd been thinking, but he couldn't actually think them, or they might turn out to be true.

"How well do you know Isabelle? Would she do something like this? The paperwork says the items were delivered to her address."

Roman's jaw worked, his secretary's words leaving a bitter taste in his mouth. "I don't think so, but here's the evidence, right?" He lifted the papers, trying to hide the disappointment that overwhelmed him all of a sudden. He'd thought she was the one, the one he could spend the rest of his life with.

Shirley leaned forward and locked her eyes with Roman's. "Just be careful when you question her. For all we know, the card was just found from an online purchase along the way. Don't make it so you can't work together anymore."

Roman nodded curtly, and Shirley turned to leave. A part of him still hoped Isabelle didn't have anything to do with this, that she really did like him. But a bigger part of him knew how people could manipulate situations and people, making him feel like a prat for even believing someone could like him for him, especially with his flaws. All women wanted was money.

He called Sam to bring the car, and they drove to Isabelle's flat. After walking up to the third floor, he stood in front of her door and knocked, the sound echoing in the empty hallway. After a few seconds, the door opened, and a woman Roman didn't recognize stood there. Her eyes went wide for a moment before turning into a bored expression.

"May I help you?" she asked, folding her arms across her middle.

"I'm here to see Isabelle. Is she in?"

The door opened a crack more, and Isabelle beamed at him. "Roman. I didn't expect to see you here today. Come in."

The other woman frowned. "I have friends coming over, so make it quick." She disappeared through a door at the back.

Isabelle looked at him with an apology written on her face. "I'm so sorry. She's not the most agreeable person in the world."

"It's a wonder you've lived with her for this long." Roman heard the stiffness in his voice, and Isabelle's eyes narrowed as if sensing his mood.

"I hope it won't be much longer. I've been saving for a long time, but now that I've been working with you, I see the light at the end of the tunnel." She grinned and bounced on her toes. Taking a step forward, she touched her hand to his, and the tingle it sent up his arm made him even angrier. She was padding her pockets and had probably manipulated him the entire time. Had she known who he was on the bus and had spilled the tea on purpose?

Shaking his head, he hoped he hadn't been duped that long. "I came by because there has been some discrepancy noted on the card I gave you. Have you used it for anything other than the materials needed for the property in London?" His voice was gruff, and he saw the fright on her face.

"No. I haven't used it since the open house in London. Shirley gave me the other one before I left for Paris."

"Can I see the card?"

She nodded and moved out of the room. Roman took in the room, noting what looked like several new pieces of furniture and décor. From what he'd known about Isabelle's situation before she started working for him, she didn't have the capital to buy all of this at once.

Isabelle returned from the back room, holding a lime-green wallet. She opened it and pulled out a few cards, panicked movements setting in after a few seconds. She stuffed a few back in and checked some of the other slots, still coming up with nothing. "I'll be right back. Maybe it fell out and into my purse."

Roman took a seat on the couch, feeling the stiffness of them. Was she trying to hide this from him? The idea of it burned inside him, and he wasn't sure what to do about it. Several minutes ticked by, and he pulled out his phone, trying to take his mind from it.

By the time she came out, Roman was convinced she was either hiding something or she'd scoured the entire flat.

With a somber expression, she walked out, extending the card to him. "Here it is." Her words were tight and forced.

He wasn't sure what to ask her next as he took the card and examined it. The numbers were the same as the report he'd read that morning, and his heart sank. Looking around the room, he asked, "Did you just refurnish this place?"

Isabelle shrugged, sitting down in one of the armchairs. "My roommate had a bunch of stuff brought in. I didn't know she was in the market to switch things out. The other furniture she had before was still in good condition."

Realization dawned on Roman, and he suddenly felt guilty for thinking it was Isabelle who'd nicked money from the company. His heart rate sped up, and he just hoped she wouldn't hold his quick assumption against him forever.

"You mentioned before that you don't get along all that well, right?"

With a quick laugh, Isabelle said, "That's an understatement. But it's hard to find an affordable place to rent here in the city, and without a car, it's easier to be close to transportation."

"Did you tell her you were doing some work for me?" He said it calmly, holding back the urge to call the authorities and report the stolen money.

Shaking her head, Isabelle said, "No. But the walls aren't all that thick between our rooms. She probably heard me talk about it with my sister."

Holding up the card, he said, "I think she used the card to buy all this." He motioned to all the furniture and then turned his gaze back to Isabelle. Her eyes were wide and her mouth open in shock.

"I found the card on the bathroom floor, which I thought was odd. I never take my purse in there." She paused for a moment, thinking it over. "You came over here because you thought it was me who took the money, didn't you?" Her eyes pleaded with him to deny it, but he couldn't.

"Honestly, I didn't know what to think. I get people trying to get close to me all the time to get access to my money, and I didn't want it to happen again. I came, knowing you'd give me an honest answer. From your look of innocence and the sight of new furniture here, I think your roommate did it."

Isabelle bit her bottom lip, her eyes blinking faster than he'd ever seen, as if it were helping her think. "We should probably report her, then." Her chest heaved, and he could see a flash of fire in her eyes. "I can't believe you thought I would steal from you."

Raising his hands, he said, "I didn't know for sure, and when Shirley investigated—"

"Shirley sent you here?"

His back bristling at her tone, he said, "Yes. The accountants found the charges and sent them to her. She looked into them, and they were mostly for furniture and décor items. Since the delivery address was here, I just wanted to come and let you explain."

Nodding, she said, "Well, thank you for doing that. I appreciate you not jumping to the wrong conclusions so quickly. But if you'll excuse me, I need to pack some things."

"Where will you go?" Roman asked, standing. The sudden realization that he might lose her hit him like a punch to the gut, and he hoped it wouldn't happen.

"I still have work to do in Paris. I'll figure out what to do about my living arrangements when I get back."

Stepping in front of her, Roman said, "I have several apartment openings. You could live in one of those." He paused for a moment and then said, "Will you have dinner with me tonight?"

She took a step back, folding her arms and narrowing her eyes. "You come over and almost accuse me of mishandling company funds, and now you want to go to dinner?"

Roman chose his words carefully, reaching his hands out for her. "I apologize for that. I never actually believed it would be you. I just wanted to get to the bottom of things and resolve it. Please, go to dinner with me?"

The moments stretched out, and his stomach sank. When she finally said, "Yes," it took a moment for him to realize she'd agreed.

"Really? Okay, I'll get us a table somewhere."

"I'm not dressing up, so it better not be somewhere fancy."

Roman studied her face and realized she was serious. All of the options that were his go-to restaurants were off the table, and he would have to get creative. "No problem. I'll pick you up at seven."

On his way out the door, he dialed the bank. When someone answered, he said, "Hello, I'd like to report a stolen card."

CHAPTER 29

Isabelle finished applying her mascara and stood back, looking at herself in the mirror. Picking up one of the lip balms her sister had requested she try out, she applied it and rubbed her lips together, liking the feel of it. The smell wasn't bad either, and since it didn't have any tint to it, Isabelle didn't have to worry about matching it to her t-shirt and jeans.

She'd pulled her hair half up and curled the ends lightly, making herself look presentable but not appearing that she'd tried too hard. When she thought of Roman, she was still somewhat bugged by the fact that he'd even think she would do something to him, but after thinking it through completely, how could he not assume? Her flatmate had everything delivered to their flat, and it was bought with the card he'd given her.

Pushing those feelings aside, she was determined to have fun tonight. Make it a good time before she had to fly back to Paris to finish out the work there. She wondered what she would do after that job had finished. It would probably be best to reach out to some of the people she'd come to know during her time with Darcy. Even if they only had a referral or two, that was better than just waiting around, hoping the work would come to her.

It might be best to stay away from working with Roman for a bit, just in case something like her flatmate stealing a credit card and buying things for the flat happened again. Even now, Isabelle wondered what kind of person would buy new furniture with a stolen company card.

She could understand how tiresome it would be to have people begging Roman for access to his money, whether it was through favors or actual work, and she didn't want him to get that impression from her. She was so grateful for all he'd done to help her get started, to have the confidence to go out on her own after she'd been fired. Now was the time to prove she could make it work with or without Roman's help. Silvain could be a good reference to start with.

The bell rang, and Isabelle walked down the hall, grateful her flatmate wasn't home. Every time she looked at the furniture now, she had a sense of guilt, that if she'd just checked on the card all the time, she wouldn't be in this mess in the first place.

Opening the door, her breath caught in her throat. She hadn't seen Roman dressed down before. The most casual he'd been was a pair of slacks and a polo shirt. Seeing him in jeans that looked like they were made for him, as well as a t-shirt that emphasized his physique, she smiled, and he did the same.

"You look beautiful, as always." Roman's grin widened, and she smiled, trying to fight the irritation she still felt about the whole situation. "Are you ready?"

"Yep. Let me get my bag, and we can head out." She walked back and grabbed the bag from her room. After locking the front door and placing the keys back into her purse, they started walking downstairs.

"Are you all right?" Roman asked from a few stairs down.

She stopped on the stair, closing her eyes tight. Did she want to go over this with him?

"I'm still bugged that you thought I could steal from you. I even called you about an upgrade on those knobs, getting your approval."

Roman frowned, a deep crease forming in his forehead. "Honestly, Isabelle. I'm sorry about that. I should have thought it through more than I did, but when everything lined up as though it was pointing to you, I tried to reserve my suspicions. I planned something tonight in the hopes that you'll forgive me."

"Are you going to do something about my flatmate?" Isabelle asked, folding her arms across her chest. His comments had already disarmed her somewhat, and she wasn't quite ready to let the bitterness go yet.

Nodding, he said, "I gave the information to the bank and my legal team, but it's her first offense, so I doubt much will come of it."

"What about the guy who took money from the townhouses in London? Did you ever figure out what to do with him?" She watched as several emotions played out on his face.

"Actually, he's been taken into custody for fraud. Seems that's happened a lot lately."

Frowning, Isabelle said, "The fraud, or the taken into custody part?" She could hear the sass in her voice and clamped her mouth shut. Neither of these were his fault but for some reason, she needed him to know she wasn't over it yet.

"Fraud." His mouth moved into a tight line. "There's only so much I can do, Isabelle."

At least he'd done something about the whole situation.

Feeling a little more relaxed, she decided to start a new conversation with, "What's our plan for tonight?"

With a mischievous grin, he said, "It's a surprise."

"You won't even give me a little clue?" For some reason when he said surprise, it called up the memory of her saying it before their driving lesson. It now left a bitter taste on her tongue.

They moved down the stairs and into the evening air. It was perfect, not quite hot or cold, but just in the middle of summer and fall.

Shaking his head, he said, "No way. It will be more fun this way."

Sam opened the back door, and for some reason, that irked her. As much of a fear as he had of driving, she just wished Roman would drive, that it could be just the two of them tonight. If she had a car, she'd even drive. He could at least open the door for her himself instead of having his driver do it.

She sat in the back of the car, and Roman slid in behind her, the excited energy seeming to stream from him, though he did look slightly concerned at her coolness. He didn't have to say anything to Sam, who took off driving down the street. They hadn't gone far when the car stopped.

Roman slipped out of the car first and then reached for her hand. "I'm going to put this on you if you don't mind." He held up a large handkerchief and raised his eyebrows, waiting for her response.

"Oh great. Are you planning a ransom or something? I don't think you'd get much out of the deal." She stepped out and turned around so he could tie it around her head.

"I think you're well worth the effort. But no, I'm not kidnapping you. I just want to see your face when we get there."

"Where?" she asked, moving the bottom section of the handkerchief so she could speak. And breathe.

Roman slipped his hand around her upper arm, gently guiding her through some grass. She'd seen they were at a park near her flat, but other than that, everything had looked ordinary. Every so often, he would stop her and give her directions, whether it was to step higher to go up a slight incline or to pull her to the side, effectively confusing her.

He finally stopped and took off the blindfold, smiling as he stepped to the side.

She saw a large blanket with a picnic basket placed on top. The tree next to it was lit up with small twinkle lights, and Isabelle couldn't help but smile.

"You did all this?" she asked, looking at him while pointing to the blanket and tree.

"I had a little help, but it was all my idea."

Isabelle smirked. "Not even from the internet?"

Roman wrinkled his nose. "Okay, maybe a little bit."

"Well, I love it. Thank you." Taking a few steps toward the blanket, she sat down on one corner and watched as he unpacked the basket.

"I'm no chef, so I got a few things at the store before I came. Turkey sandwich?" He handed her a wrapped sandwich and pulled out some crisps and two bottles of soda. "For dessert, we have some crêpes from a French vendor I found downtown. I just hope they'll still be warm by the time we eat them."

Staring at him for a moment, Isabelle was grateful for this time, even though it had started from a spilled cup of tea. Leaning in, she placed a hand on his and locked eyes with him. "Thank you. No one's ever done anything like this for me before." The thought that had gone into this helped melt her frustrations about the card mix-up, and she breathed in, helping her muscles to relax some.

Giving her the half-smile that made her stomach flip every time, he shrugged. "When you said I couldn't take you somewhere fancy, I had to get creative. This is my first picnic."

"Ever?"

He nodded, laughing a bit.

"I'm honored to be with you on your first picnic. What do you think?" She looked up at him, wondering what his childhood had been like if he'd never eaten in a park.

"It's not bad. It's a little awkward not having something to rest the food on, but I do like not being bothered with waiters."

Shaking her head, she took a bite of the sandwich. There were perks to hanging out with a billionaire, and this was no ordinary store-bought sandwich. The explosion of flavor filled her mouth, and each bite was better than the last.

They watched the sun go down and leaned back to stare at the stars. After chatting for some time, Roman stood and reached out his hand for her. "We should probably get you home. I don't want you to go without sleep when you leave tomorrow. What time is the flight?"

"Eight."

"You booked it for first class, right? I'd offer my jet, but I have to fly to Scotland tomorrow." Roman cocked his head to the side and gave her a stern look.

"Shirley booked it for me. I'm sure she would adhere to your crazy requests. It's a short flight. I'm fine sitting in the regular section."

Roman gathered the blanket, tucking it under one arm. He picked up the picnic basket, and they started walking back to the car. With both of their hands swinging so close to one another, a thrill shot through her when he caught hers in his and he interlaced his fingers. He'd done it without looking, as if not wanting to make a big deal about it. But it was to Isabelle.

The mixture of excitement and hope wound through her like a spring, and she suddenly wanted this night to last forever. The fact that he'd done all this as an apology, an activity he'd never done before, softened her irritation towards him.

Once they drove back to her flat, they stood at her door as she pulled out the keys. Looking up at him, she said, "Thank you for tonight."

He reached out for her shoulders, and his eyes bored into hers. "No, thank you. I'm sorry about earlier, and just know I am grateful to you for all you've done. Besides," he said, running a hand through her hair. "I like being around you. You make me want to be better." His eyes held hers, his gaze tender, before they dropped to her lips.

The tension sparked between them, and Isabelle waited for him to lean forward and kiss her, but with a wry smile, he turned and headed down the stairs. She wasn't sure what had caused his sudden departure, but as far as dates went, this one was at the top of her list, passing any Aaron or her past boyfriends had even attempted. They'd had their struggles over the past few weeks, but she hoped they'd be able to get things back on track and moving forward.

CHAPTER 30

*I*sabelle packed up the next morning, and Sam took her to the airport where she flew first class to Paris. It was nice that Roman would've had Sam fly her in his jet had it been available, but she was almost grateful for some sense of normalcy in riding in a regular airplane and having to push through crowds to get to her gate.

Once in Paris, she hired a car to take her to the property. On the way over, she looked down at her hand, realizing that the ring line she'd had on her third finger had colored in, looking the same as the rest.

What had she been thinking when she'd agreed to be Aaron's fiancé? And why had she said she was Roman's to Monsieur Guilbert? They'd hardly known each other at the time. But now, more than ever, she wished she had a ring from Roman instead.

The fixtures had been delivered, and Isabelle pulled out a tall ladder, one that she'd instructed the contractor to leave for her. She could have instructed the guy to install them, but she liked seeing things come together, and at the moment, she needed something to do that didn't consist of hanging out in the flat where her flatmate had stolen her boss's credit card and charged several thousand pounds. She also didn't want to stay in London, afraid that she'd just mess up again and it would be the end of her chances with Roman.

Holding up the small fixture, she worked to screw it all together, making sure the light bulbs worked before putting the glass bowl into place. She'd finished everything but the large ceiling fan when she heard a knock at the door.

"Roman, what are you—Oh, hello, Charlotte. I'm surprised to see you here."

The older woman smiled and nodded, her small purse dangling from her crossed arms. "I was just here visiting one of the families on the other side of the street. They said things went smoothly here, and they're excited about the upgrades to their property."

"That will be the next step, I think. I'm almost finished with this side. Just putting the finishing touches on them, and then families can start moving in." Isabelle worked her way back down the ladder, not wanting to topple over while she wasn't actively putting something on the ceiling.

The woman caught her hand and looked at Isabelle, eyes wide. "What happened, dear?"

Isabelle's mind churned, trying to decide what to say to the sweet older woman. "I just take it off when I'm doing a lot of the design work. I worry that it will get caught in something or will get ruined somehow."

"You're sure there's nothing wrong between the two of you?" Charlotte's eyes narrowed, and Isabelle took in a breath.

"No, we're doing well. Roman is on his way to Scotland today. I already kind of miss him." As much as she told herself she was saying these things for show, she knew deep down that she really did miss him.

Patting her hand, the woman said, "Well, if you ever need

to talk after an argument or misunderstanding, I'm your girl. Sometimes men can be a bit hardheaded, and it can be so frustrating. I went through a lot before I married Silvain."

"What happened?" She'd piqued her curiosity, and Isabelle motioned to a chair and a bucket, sitting down on the latter.

After Charlotte took a seat on the chair, she smiled and shook her head. "That man seemed to be the slowest at realizing how I felt about him. He'd taken his father's business and grown it significantly quite a while before we met. Well, with money comes a lot of crazy people out of the woodwork, trying to get something. It took a while to convince him I was there for him and not for his money."

"How'd you do that exactly?"

"A tragedy happened in the family. His brother was killed in a car accident, and the family had a hard time dealing with the loss. I brought over meals and just stayed to listen whenever I could, not necessarily thinking it was for anything other than to help soothe a wound. Silvain realized I wasn't going to run when things got hard, and we started dating." Her grin turned mischievous. "We got married three months later. Forty-two years is a long time, dear, but it takes work on both sides. At least you're already engaged."

Isabelle tried to choke back the tears, knowing Charlotte would be suspicious and ask questions. She finally squeaked out, "Yeah, that's true."

"Well, I better get going. I have some food in the oven at home that needs to be finished off for dinner. Good luck, and I'll see you soon, Isabelle." The lady moved in to kiss each cheek, and as she took a step back, she squeezed Isabelle's upper arms, giving her a smile of encouragement.

Staring at the door long after she left, Isabelle tried to understand how she felt about the man with the scar, realizing her feelings went much deeper than she'd thought. The curve of his lips, the way his scar pulled at the corner of his eye when he smiled. The way he treated her like a lady, opening doors and pushing in chairs. Not to mention the feel of his lips on hers. All of it sent shivers through her, and he wasn't even in the room.

Picking up her phone, she thought about calling him, wondering if she should tell him her feelings now. No, it was better to wait, to talk about it face-to-face.

Clicking her phone on, she saw a text message from him.

I hope you made it to Paris safely. I can't wait to see you again soon.

Isabelle hoped that meant he had feelings for her too and not that she was just another employee or contractor his company employed.

Clicking on her contacts, she called Juliette, ready for a night out.

CHAPTER 31

Isabelle had spent a quiet night in the hotel room, as Juliette wasn't able to meet until the following day. With skin care sales up a significant amount since hiring Tristan to advertise for the company, Juliette was working to hire more people to help cover the influx.

Now, waiting for a table to open up at their favorite restaurant, Juliette and Isabelle chatted about little things, helping to relieve some of the pressure she'd felt over the past few days.

"How goes hiring the world?" Isabelle said with a bit of sarcasm.

"Ugh. You'd think people would learn how to read all of the instructions and follow them accordingly. In my ad, I asked for a one-page resume and a couple of references. One lady sent me a booklet of her life story."

Isabelle laughed. "No way. Really?"

Juliette rolled her eyes. "Yes. I made it through one page and decided to put it in the trash. I know it sounds harsh, but I don't have time to go through twenty pages of 'and then' just to see if you qualify for this job. And if you can't complete the one thing I asked, then you might as well go somewhere else."

"Brava. I'm liking this spunky streak you've got going on."

"And it seems you took over my reserved trait, at least today anyway. What's up?" Juliette pulled a piece of hair away from Isabelle's face, making it so she couldn't hide behind it.

The more Isabelle thought about the role reversal, the more it seemed to click. Juliette had always had long hair, using it to shade the horrendous acne she'd battled with from pre-puberty. Isabelle had always been able to speak about everything to everyone, but for some reason, she didn't feel like talking at all at the moment.

Shrugging, she said, "I think I like Roman."

Juliette smiled wide but curbed it a bit and asked, "What's wrong with that?"

"I don't think it will work. He's in charge of this huge company. He could practically swim through all the money he has, and I'm just the daughter of an artist who's a little lost."

"Please! You've started to build your own company, and who's to say it won't be international soon?"

"My flatmate stole his business card from my wallet and bought all new furniture for the flat."

They were escorted to their table, and when Juliette pressed her for more information, Isabelle divulged the whole story, even the part about accusing Roman of thinking it could have been her.

Chewing on a piece of bread, Juliette finally said, "So you're a bit conflicted, then?"

Isabelle let out a laugh, even though there was nothing funny about it. She'd kept all of these feelings bottled up for so long that it was either laugh or cry.

"What is it you're worried about? Besides the money thing."

"That I'll fall for him and the same thing that happened with Aaron will happen again." Taking a bite of her salad, Isabelle chewed slowly, trying to push away the niggling feeling that that was her future.

Juliette's mouth went slack, and she tapped Isabelle's hand. When Isabelle turned in the direction she was pointing, Isabelle's expression mirrored her sister's, seeing someone she hadn't seen in weeks striding toward their table.

Aaron Hill.

"What are you doing here?" she asked, staring up at him with hooded eyes.

With the arrogance he'd always carried, he pulled a chair from the table next to theirs and scooted it closer to Isabelle than she felt comfortable with.

"I've been trying to track you down for days. I finally had to resort to waiting for your sister to lead me to you."

"You've been stalking me to get to her?" Juliette's face hardened, and Isabelle could feel the tension thicken. "I'm glad she didn't marry you after all. You're a piece of work." Wiping off her mouth, Juliette turned to Isabelle. "I'm going to freshen up. I'll be back in a moment."

Her expression seemed to warn Isabelle of something, but after weeks of reminiscing over her relationship with Aaron, she knew what she'd felt had only been a surface attraction. It had all come out of her insecurity to find someone to spend forever with when she should have been more worried about developing herself so she could find the person who would match her correctly.

And at that moment, all she wanted was to tell Roman how she felt, that she was in love with him.

"You seem to be a jet setter, my Issy. It took a while to find out you'd moved back to Paris."

"I'm not living in Paris. I'm working here." She scooted her chair away, not wanting to even touch the man. His face didn't hold the same attraction that had once pulled her toward him, and she wished she could go back and change a lot of things about her past.

He trailed a finger up her arm, and she shivered, her gag reflex getting ready to react. "I've heard you're working for Magnolia Property Group. I always knew you had a future in design."

Standing, she grabbed her purse and moved toward the door of the restaurant, not worried that she hadn't even gotten the chance to eat her meal. Her appetite was gone now anyway. Juliette would understand her need to abandon her.

She'd made it a few steps from the entrance when a hand caught her arm and pulled her to a stop.

"Please, Issy. Just listen to me."

"It's Isabelle."

He laughed. "In two months' time, you're now Isabelle. Tell me, what happened to you?"

"I realized that I deserve better than you. All you ever did was tear me down to keep me in one spot, to mold me into what you wanted. But I've found someone who rejoices in my talents and is grateful for what I do."

Nodding, as if not believing her, Aaron said, "Well, what if I came to say I made a mistake, that I want you back?"

Juliette came out at that moment, and Isabelle was grateful for the support. "I don't want you. I'm in love with someone else."

CHAPTER 32

After the quick trip to Scotland, Roman asked Shirley to cancel the rest of his meetings the next day. Sam prepared the plane again, and they flew to Paris, with Roman anxious to surprise Isabelle. He wanted to spend more time with her, felt an attraction or a pull he hadn't felt in a long time, if ever.

Arriving at the Paris property, he walked into one of the units, calling out for her. He tried unit after unit, and it wasn't until one of the workers told him she'd left for lunch that he walked back to the car.

He didn't know much about where she might be, and not wanting to tip her off, he texted Tristan.

She and Juliette are at Café de Flore for lunch. Come see me when you're done. I have some new things to discuss about your marketing.

Roman was grateful for the quick messaging from his friend and gave Sam the address to the café. He looked around, realizing it might be better to take some kind of present. After their picnic the other night, he'd had a hard time getting her out of his mind, and he realized he wanted something more. He was finally ready to take the leap and have a relationship. She'd never shuddered in his presence, and from everything she'd done to help him over the past several weeks, he didn't want to lose her to anything.

"Sam, stop over there. I just want to get something for her, and then I'll walk from here."

Turning around in the driver's seat, Sam smiled at him, "Good luck, sir. I hope things turn out as you hope they will."

He hadn't mentioned anything specific, but Sam had to know how Roman felt about the girl with long brown hair and eyes that could see into his soul.

"Thanks, Sam. I hope so too. I'll text you when I need you."

Sam tipped his hat and walked away.

Roman thought about the Isabelle again, walking up to a flower stand. He wasn't sure what kind she'd like, so he asked the woman running the stand to surprise him. With a beautiful bouquet of lilies and a few other flowers, he took longer strides, ready for the suspense to be over.

What would he say? Would it be best to start with a speech or to just say he loved her? He loved her. The words played silently on his tongue, and he felt the confirmation of it fill his body.

Turning the corner, he looked up to see the name of the café and then turned his attention to find the entrance. He saw a couple kissing and was about to turn away from them, when they pulled back, and he recognized Isabelle. Not wanting to see any more, he turned and walked back around the corner, throwing the flowers into a bin on the way past.

A tightness pulled his chest in so much that he was afraid something besides his heart would break. He should have known, should have listened to Tristan all those weeks ago. She'd just broken up with a guy, a fiancé. That must have been who was there, with his lips on her soft delicate ones.

He felt his defenses rise, sealing out the hurt he'd known would come from falling for a woman like her. Lifting his phone to his ear, he called Sam, giving him directions to where he was. He'd go see Tristan and then head back to London. Once the project was done in Paris, he'd forget about working in France, at least for a few years. He knew he'd think about her every time he was here, and that would be the cruelest part of it all.

Isabelle had to work to pull back from Aaron's kiss, as he held her upper body against his chest, making it difficult to breathe. She finally got her arms up high enough to push off, grateful for the distance between them and the air filling her lungs.

"Why would you do that? I just told you I was in love with someone else." She felt the anger ripple through her, masking the regret that she'd ever had feelings for this guy. What luck that they'd broken up before she'd been stuck with him for life.

"Because I know you've missed me. You've loved me for years, and you think that's going to change in a matter of weeks?" His glare was haughty, taunting.

Isabelle nodded. "As a matter of fact, yes. I've found someone who treats me how I deserve to be treated, not like some plaything you can cast off and then come back to whenever you please." She spat the words out, feeling lighter than she had in a long time.

"You should be grateful I'm giving us another chance. Not many girls would be so lucky." He smiled, sending chills running through Isabelle. "You need me, Issy. You've always needed me, and I realized I need you."

Searching his face, Isabelle asked, "Why the sudden change of heart? And how did you know I was working for Magnolia Property Group?"

His eyes narrowed in her direction. "Because I love you. And with your connections, I figured you could introduce me to the CEO."

Turning to walk back to their table, Isabelle couldn't stand to look at him for another moment. Juliette walked next to her, her presence giving Isabelle strength.

Aaron caught her arm, whipping her around to look at him. There was fire in his eyes, as if he were ready to throw a tantrum because he hadn't gotten what he wanted.

"Don't turn away from me," he said, his eyes narrowed.

Juliette moved between them, her chin raised. "My sister has said she no longer wants a relationship with you. I suggest you move along, or I'll dial the authorities."

Aaron stared at her, the conflicting emotions playing in his eyes. He stuck out his finger and reached over Juliette's shoulder to point at Isabelle. "Just know this is the last chance you'll get with me. You won't find yourself a better offer than me."

He turned on his heel and walked away, allowing Isabelle to breathe again.

Juliette turned, wrapping her sister in a hug and staying that way for a few moments. "Do you want to go?"

Isabelle shook her head against her sister's shoulder. "I'm hoping they haven't cleared our food yet."

The two of them laughed as they returned to their table, but Isabelle couldn't help but cast a wary glance in the direction Aaron had gone. She hoped he would give up and realize it was over. For her, it was. She'd never be luckier than if given the chance to be with Roman Hamilton. That's who her heart belonged to for the first time and forever.

* * *

AFTER FINISHING THEIR MEAL, Juliette asked Isabelle to come with her to Tristan's office, as he'd worked to create some ideas for Isabelle's design business. Ready to just go back and finish work, Isabelle dragged her feet, not sure she was in the business frame of mind right now.

They moved to the sleek building downtown and took the elevator up several floors. The look of the place was ultramodern, and there were some elements she tucked away in her mind for later, knowing that every bit of inspiration could make a room pop.

Juliette spoke to a woman at the desk, and she waved them back to what Isabelle thought was Tristan's office. It was definitely a man's workspace with the sports paraphernalia and the lack of much decoration. But a picture on the desk was of Tristan and Juliette, and Isabelle smiled. At least the one touch in the man's office was one of her sister.

"Hey, I didn't know you were stopping by," Tristan said, greeting Juliette with a kiss.

Isabelle watched them and wished Roman were here to kiss her hello. The only other kiss she thought of was the one Aaron had placed on her just an hour ago, making her cringe at the thought.

"Hi, Isabelle. How are things? Are you liking being a business owner?"

Taking a seat on one of his chairs, she said, "It's not bad, but then again, I haven't had much experience yet. I'm finishing up my first job with Roman hopefully this evening."

She didn't know if she was imagining something, but his

eyes flashed when she said Roman's name, and it piqued her curiosity.

Looking between her and Juliette, Tristan asked, "How was lunch? Anything interesting happen?" He locked eyes with Isabelle, and she squirmed a bit, feeling uncomfortable.

"Aaron, Isabelle's ex-fiancé, showed up, saying he's stalked me to track down Isa, and demanded that they get back together. When she said she was in love with someone else, he kissed her." Juliette's bitter words brought the whole memory back, and Isabelle wished she could start the day over, doing everything she could to not see him again.

Tristan shifted to lean back against his chair, his face somber as he asked, "I know it's a bit odd for me to ask you this, but may I ask who it is you love?"

"Roman." The word came out in a whisper, as if battling within herself to declare the truth of it. She'd told two people already today about the man she loved, but he himself still didn't know it.

Standing, Tristan said, "We'd better go, then, or else you'll miss him."

Isabelle turned to look at him as he stood next to the office door. "Miss who?"

"Roman. He came to surprise you and just saw the part where you were kissing another man. He came here after, pretty devastated. Sam took him to the airport, and they were going to fly back to London as soon as possible."

Isabelle's stomach clenched. She could only imagine what it had been like for Roman to walk around the corner and see her kissing another man. If only he'd stayed a few more moments, he might have been able to save her from Aaron and cement the fact that her heart belonged to another.

The three of them hopped into Tristan's Mercedes, and he pulled out of the garage and onto the streets. Isabelle was mildly impressed with his ability to maneuver around and through cars on the busy streets. She could feel the race of it all, hoping they'd be able to catch him before the plane took off.

Leaning forward, Isabelle looked at Tristan. "What did he say when he saw you? Did he say why he'd come to Paris?"

"He just said he'd had a great night with you on your picnic and that he'd realized he wanted you to be in his life. He canceled his meetings and flew over in the hopes of telling you how he felt. But then he saw your kiss with what's-his-name and decided you probably didn't feel the same."

Touching his shoulder, she urged, "Hurry, Tristan. Please hurry."

Taking out her phone, she called Roman's phone, but the call went to voicemail after two rings. She opened a text, hoping he would at least look at it before boarding the plane.

Don't take off yet. I need to see you.

Several minutes later, they'd arrived at the tarmac, and looking around, the plane had gone. She looked down at the end of the runway to see it was getting ready for takeoff right then.

Getting out of the car, she sprinted toward it, waving her hands in the air and yelling, even though the sound of the engines most likely drowned them out. She'd made it quite a ways closer before the airplane took off, speeding down the runway and then pulling into the air.

Sadness filled her, but her hope wasn't lost. He'd come all the way to Paris just to see her, no ulterior motive, no prior meeting. Just to surprise her. He had to have some feelings for her.

Looking down at her phone, she saw his name next to a text notification. Swiping her phone open, she tried not to cry as she read the words.

I'm already gone.

Once back at the car, she showed the text to Juliette before crumpling at the side of the car. Tears streamed down her face, and she wished she could go back and at least see him there, call to him and tell him how much she loved him.

"What do you think he meant by that?" she heard Juliette ask Tristan.

"I'm not exactly sure, but I assume he's building walls again. We should head over and get my plane ready to fly to London. Maybe we can catch him there."

"No." The word surprised even Isabelle as she stood, swiping at the tears running down her face. The other two looked at her as if she'd gone mad.

"What do you mean? I thought you said you loved him." Juliette's eyes looked as though Isabelle had sprouted several more heads.

Shaking her head, Isabelle straightened. "I do love him. But if he's not going to wait and let me at least explain myself this time, then what good would it do? I love the man, but I'm not going to want to have to defend myself every time there's something that isn't what it looks like."

"You're not going to try?" Tristan asked, a frown on his face.

"I'm going to finish up the property and then head home."

Juliette squinted one eye. "Home where?"

"I think I need a little time in Dinan."

CHAPTER 34

Two weeks passed, and as hard as Roman tried, he couldn't get Isabelle out of his head. He'd thrown himself into work, but the balm it usually held didn't seem to ease anything, and he wasn't sure what to do about it.

Shirley had relayed the message that Isabelle had completed the project in Paris and the company had paid her the agreed upon amount, but he hadn't heard from her in all this time, and it tore at his heart.

He didn't know what had happened as they took off from Paris until after he'd returned to London. Tristan had texted him around the time they'd touched down to say that they'd tried to catch him before the plane took off, but Roman hadn't cared why they'd tried to track him down, only avoiding calls coming from any French phone numbers.

Isabelle was probably happier anyway, going back to the guy who'd broken her heart the first time. With all she'd told him, it sounded like the guy was a loser. But Roman shouldn't have thought he had a chance with her in the first place, especially after he'd accused her of taking money from his company. Maybe that contributed to her reaction, that she hadn't fully forgiven him for it. Now he was miserable and didn't know how to fix it.

He'd taken some time to visit his sisters the weekend before, glad to be able to forget about the dismal state of his life for a few hours as he remembered his times in college. Things were so much simpler then.

Walking into his office, Shirley picked up several pieces of rubbish and threw them into the bin. Giving him a look of concern, she asked, "What's wrong with you? You've been moping for days. What can I do to help you?"

"Find me another deal to work through." He waved a hand through the air to emphasize that wasn't really going to help.

"We have that property in North London that is mostly ready for sale. It could use some staging to help the process along." Shirley's face told him she knew exactly what she was doing by baiting him.

"Okay, hire a stager. I don't care who it is. Let's just get that property sold and move on to the next." He dropped his eyes and pretended to read a paper in front of him, his eyes scanning the line three times without comprehending any of it.

Shirley didn't move, and after a few minutes of silence, Roman looked up to find her glaring at him. "Is that what you want your life to look like? What about people's memories of you? 'He just worked on one real estate deal after another, never enjoying life'?"

Not in the mood to discuss this with her, he said, "No. Did you have a reason for coming in here, Shirley?"

Tilting her head a bit, she said, "Tristan is on his way here. He's in town for meetings and insists he needs to meet with you. I'll let him in when he arrives." Turning on her heel, she left the room and shut the door with a loud click.

Rubbing his face with both hands, he hoped Tristan wasn't there about anything other than business. He'd done enough reminiscing of their college days while with the girls this past weekend, and he didn't want to talk about Isabelle.

A sliver of curiosity ran through him as he wondered if she was engaged again, for real this time, and what she'd been doing other than that. He wasn't always the one to approve the new staging process, but they hadn't really needed one for the last couple of weeks. Shaking his head, he concentrated on cleaning out his email inbox, hoping to distract himself from further heartbreak.

A knock sounded at the door several minutes later, and Tristan walked in, unbuttoning his suit coat before sitting down. He was a tall man, and even lounging back in the small office chair, it looked as though only a fraction of his body was actually sitting on it.

"To what do I owe the pleasure?" Roman said drily.

"The fact that I had meetings here and that you're an idiot."

Roman studied his face, seeing no hint of humor there. "What are you talking about? I'm just doing what I always do. Work." He waved his hands over the desk covered in papers and booklets of properties the Magnolia Property Group already owned or were interested in acquiring.

"Isabelle. You love her, don't you?" Tristan leaned forward, his elbows resting on his legs.

Shaking his head, Roman said, "I told you, man. I don't want to talk about her. She's probably set a date with that creep, and they'll get married and live happily ever after." Closing his eyes, he rubbed at his temples, feeling a headache coming on.

"If you'd just listen, you'd know that the creep is still a creep. You only saw them kiss because she'd just told him that she was in love with someone else. You. She loves you.

Or loved you. She's been pretty cold about the whole thing since, or so Juliette tells me."

"How do I know that's not just some story she conjured up?"

Tristan frowned, a deep line forming in his forehead. "Really? After all Isabelle has done for you, this is how you're going to act? I'm sorry, man. I know you're one of my best friends, but I've got to tell you, I'm on Isabelle's team right now." He shrugged his shoulders and pursed his lips, about as angry as Roman had ever seen him. "Juliette was standing right there as Isabelle said it. Or is Juliette in on the conspiracy too? But if you really loved Isabelle, you'd trust any story she told you."

Guilt seeped into Roman's stomach, a bitter taste rising in his throat and mouth. His mind spun with the information. How could he have screwed things up again? If only his pride hadn't pulled him away in Paris, he might have known exactly what was going on with the situation. He just hoped there was a way Isabelle would forgive him. "Why did you wait so long to tell me all this?"

Throwing his hands up in the air, Tristan said, "Really? You haven't answered any of my calls since. I didn't want to explain it all in a text or email, so I knew I'd just have to tell you in person."

"Do you think I messed things up beyond repair?" Roman held his breath, hoping Tristan wouldn't confirm it.

"No, but if you don't act soon, she'll write you off completely. She was in Dinan for a week after the Paris job was finished, and she returned here recently. I can't believe you haven't tried to see her."

Rolling his eyes, Roman said, "Now that you've made me feel sufficiently chastised, I need to figure out a plan. If she's going to forgive me, I'm going to have to do something to prove that I'm an idiot, but one who loves her."

The first genuine smile crossed Tristan's face since he'd walked into Roman's office. "Now you're talking. What do you have in mind?"

CHAPTER 35

*I*sabelle unpacked the last of her boxes, grateful for a clean slate now that she'd come home from Dinan. Her flatmate wasn't there, and Isabelle wasn't sure if she'd been arrested for her crimes or if she was just out with friends like always.

Isabelle had been able to find a small place a few streets over. The price was almost double what she'd been paying at the other flat, but it was worth it to live by herself for a while. She'd felt so much better after coming back from her parents' home, and although they encouraged her to stay there or to move to Paris, Isabelle knew she needed to go back to London. She'd already received several phone calls from other agents who'd found her through her website, and she wasn't going to give up her staging business just because another British guy had broken her heart.

After lining up another staging job that would begin in a few days, she was trying to stay optimistic that she wasn't out of options after these next few jobs and destined to be an assistant for something she loved.

It had been almost three weeks since Aaron had shown

up, and Roman had stopped speaking to her. As much as she wished she could stop looking at her phone with the small hope that it would be him contacting her, her heart refused to get behind her brain.

A knock sounded, and Isabelle paused, unsure what to do. The only people who knew she now lived here were her family and her flatmate so she could forward any mail.

Several seconds passed, and the knock sounded again, louder this time, more urgent. Walking to the door, she brushed a lock of hair away from her mouth and opened it. Surprise knocked her back a step as she saw Sam standing there.

"How did you find me?" she asked, folding her arms and looking behind him to the hall. Roman wasn't there. But Sam was his minion, and she wasn't sure what could bring him to her door this early in the afternoon.

One corner of his mouth turned up, the most expression she'd ever seen from him before. "We had a client bring a gift by the office for you. I have strict instructions to take you to retrieve it."

"I'm not going to step another foot in Roman's office, so you can tell him to keep it himself." The words came flying out, making her feel some relief from the pent-up frustration that had been brewing the past few weeks. She just wished it was Roman standing in front of her so she could release it completely.

"It's not in Mr. Hamilton's office. Please just come with me, Miss Rousseau. It will make both of our lives easier."

Isabelle wasn't sure about that, but then again, her curiosity was making it difficult to say no. "Let me change." She'd been working in these clothes for the past two days, trying to organize her place, and hadn't seen anyone, so she hadn't been ashamed to wear it over again.

"I'll be downstairs when you're ready." Sam turned even

before she'd shut the door and moved down the hall toward the stairs.

Racing to the bathroom, she took a quick shower and then dressed in clean clothes before pulling her hair into a messy bun. She wasn't in the mood to try and impress anyone, only taking a few seconds to add some mascara before grabbing her purse and moving out of the flat.

As she walked down to the street, she saw the same car she'd ridden in so many times, and thoughts of Roman filled her mind. Pushing them to the side, she just hoped he wasn't the surprise, sitting inside waiting for her.

She'd wondered what she'd do if he ever apologized for just taking off and not hearing her side of the story, but as the days dragged on, she knew he wasn't about to do that.

Sam stood outside the car, holding the door open for her. He placed his forefinger and thumb on the brim of his driver hat and tipped it at her.

She nodded and slipped inside, grateful for its emptiness and large space. She pulled out her phone but saw no notifications. Dropping it into her bag, she leaned back as the car started moving.

After several minutes, she called up to Sam and asked, "Is it far, Sam?"

He shook his head and said nothing. A man of so many words.

Isabelle sat back and watched the scenery pass, not consciously thinking of much until they pulled up to one of the parking lots in downtown London. When the car stopped, she straightened.

"What are we doing here, Sam?" What was going on? Who was this client, and why was she here?

Instead of speaking, he got out of the car and moved to her door, holding it open for her. He kept his head bowed but held out an envelope for her. Shutting the door after she exited, he got back in the car and pulled away, driving down the road.

Opening the envelope, she pulled out a card and read the contents of it.

The Royal Ballet requests the presence of Miss Isabelle Rousseau on this the twenty-third of September to participate in a dress rehearsal. Please report to the door on Bow Street for entry.

Isabelle's mouth dropped open, and she read it over twice more, not sure she was reading it correctly. Other than her family, she couldn't remember who she'd told that seeing a performance of the Royal Ballet was a dream of hers, and they didn't have the connections to pull off this sort of thing. Well, maybe Tristan, and he would do anything for Juliette. Had she arranged this?

Moving in the direction of the door, she was hustled in and given a leotard and tights. Butterflies erupted in her stomach, wondering if that was what she'd need to be wearing to watch them rehearse.

The next hour and a half went by like it was only minutes, and Isabelle couldn't help but hold the wide grin on her face the entire time. Seeing the grace of the dancers, their poise and precision with each of the movements, had her in awe of their abilities.

They'd actually invited Isabelle to practice with them and assigned a few of the dancers to her, helping her with the routine and adjusting her technique, which was rusty from so many years since her injury. When the choreographer announced they were done until that evening, Isabelle wished she could stay and do this every day.

Once she'd finished and showered, changing back into her street clothes, several of the dancers approached her with a large bouquet of deep red roses.

One of the girls handed them to her and another gave her a card, both their faces mischievous with grins.

"What are these for?" Isabelle asked, hoping to understand the situation. She'd been given the most amazing opportunity by dancing with these ladies, but to receive such a large number of beautiful flowers? It didn't seem like it was in her realm of luck to get both in one day.

"Someone dropped them off and told us to give them to you after rehearsal. Go on. Open the card."

The other girl bumped the first with her elbow. "Let her do it. It's her bouquet."

Isabelle giggled and slipped her finger through the envelope flap, noting it was much longer than a regular note for flowers. Pulling out the note, she read aloud so the girls could hear. "Please accept this ticket to see the show tonight as a thank you for all you've done for me."

Turning the card over, she saw no signs of who it could be from. Sticking her hand back into the envelope, she pulled out a ticket for the show that night at the Royal Opera House. Behind it were several fifty-pound notes and a note that said, "Visit the dress shop three streets down."

She looked up at the girls and narrowed her eyes. "You're sure you don't know who dropped off all of this?"

Both girls shook their heads, no sign of hiding anything evident on their faces. One finally spoke up. "Are you going to go? There's a little more than two hours before the show begins. You could find something and get ready before coming back."

Taking a moment to think it over, Isabelle figured she may as well go through with it. Part of her worried about not having anyone to enjoy it with, but it was too short of notice to fly Juliette in for it.

Walking out of the building, Isabelle located the dress shop on the map on her phone and started in that direction, trying to hang on to the large bouquet and keep her mind from wondering who would do such things.

CHAPTER 36

*I*sabelle left the dress shop feeling more glamorous than she had in, well, ever. The ladies must have received advance notice that she'd be in, because they already had several dresses picked out that were close to her size. Sending her next to a beautician shop two doors down, Isabelle's hair was piled on top of her head in curls, her makeup applied, and jewelry placed.

After several attempts to get the women to speak of the person who'd set it all up, she decided to enjoy being pampered and worry about it later.

Now, in one of the booths that hung nearest the stage, Isabelle settled in with a few other people, an empty seat next to her. As she thought about all of the things that had happened today, from dancing with the ballet company for rehearsal to seeing the show as well, the moment she'd shared those dreams with Roman flashed before her mind.

Did he do all of this? A chill ran up her spine, and her whole body shivered in reaction.

A hand lightly touched her shoulder just as the lights were dimming, and when she looked up, she saw Roman's face, sending her pulse racing. He slid into the seat next to her, staring at her in the dim light.

"Did you arrange all of this?" She circled her finger around as if that could signify all of the joy she'd felt throughout the day.

He nodded, giving her a close-lipped smile. "I knew I'd screwed up, more than I wanted to admit at first. So I had to figure out a way to make it up to you, to prove how much I really trust you."

"Trust. Is that all you feel toward me?" she asked, fighting to keep her voice to a whisper.

Shaking his head, he said, "No, Isabelle. I love you. These past weeks without you have been miserable, and everyone has made note of it, asking where you've been. I just want you to know that I'm terribly sorry I didn't speak to you about the situation. I should have just asked you about it instead of being a coward and running away. Will you forgive me?" He'd said the words so quickly that his chest was rising and falling quickly.

Isabelle had heard only stitches of what he'd said, understanding most of it as her brain honed in on the first few words he'd said. *Isabelle, I love you.*

"You love me?" she asked, leaning closer so he could hear over the opening music of the orchestra below them.

"More than I thought I could ever love someone."

She leaned next to his ear so he could hear over the commotion. "I love you too, Roman."

She pulled back enough to see his eyes and saw he was near tears. Leaning forward, she wrapped her arms around him, holding on tighter than she had to anything before.

He pushed her back somewhat, and his lips brushed hers, soft at first and then deepening in intensity, as if trying to make up for all the kisses they'd missed in the past few weeks.

Taking a breath, she leaned into him as they gazed down at the stage where the first few dancers worked through the movements she'd practiced with them a couple of hours before. Turning up to look at him, she whispered, "I can't believe you remembered this. The practice with the company and seeing them perform here in the Royal Opera House. This is a night I will never forget."

He smiled at her. "It was your dream, and for some reason, it stuck out to me when you said it." He paused for a moment before continuing. "I've been working on conquering my fear as well, and I have you to thank for it."

She brought her eyebrows together, not quite sure where this was going.

He laughed softly and took her hand in his, the feel of it warm and lightly callused. He raised his other hand, holding a hat similar to the one Sam used when he drove the limo. "I'm the one who drove the car here this afternoon."

"Really? It was smooth, as if Sam had been driving it." She felt as though the emotions were going to explode from her as she realized the magnitude of his confession.

"Tristan was my coach when he was here a few days ago. He might have an ulcer now, but at least we made it through the worst of my fears."

"Fears?"

He paused for several seconds before saying, "I thought I'd lost you forever. That fear was a hundred times worse than worrying I was going to die in a car accident."

"I'd say you know how to say sorry by now." Leaning closer, she whispered, "Thank you."

Reaching up and touching her hand to his cheek, she kissed him softly, savoring the moment as her dream was fulfilled and she wasn't alone.

EPILOGUE

Two months later, Roman and Isabelle flew to California for a trip. Roman wanted to show her where he'd gone to school and have her meet some of the people who'd changed his life for the better.

When she spoke to Mrs. Montgomery, the wife of Roman's frat house mentor who had passed away, Isabelle could tell why this family was such a big part of Roman's past. Their warmth and generosity made it feel like she was home, even though her loving family was across the world.

Talking with her daughter Penny in the kitchen after a long day of sightseeing and reminiscing, Isabelle felt at peace with the world.

"So, have you and Roman talked about marriage?" Penny asked, her curiosity reminding Isabelle of her own at that age.

With a giggle, Isabelle said, "In passing, yes. But nothing concrete. I was engaged to someone else just a few months ago."

"But you love him, right?"

"Of course. Way more than I ever loved the other guy."

Penny grinned. "What if he proposed today? What would you say?"

Isabelle thought about it for a moment, and when the word *yes* crossed her mind, she felt the confirmation of it flow through her. "I would accept."

"Really?" Roman's voice startled her, causing her to turn and look at him standing there in pyjama bottoms and a t-shirt.

Isabelle only faintly realized Penny had slipped out of the room, leaving the two of them with the stillness in the air around them.

She nodded slowly, not sure what to think about this whole conversation. They'd only known each other for five months. With it being the week before Christmas, she hadn't expected any of this kind of talk for quite some time, let alone around the holidays.

He took her hand, silently leading her out to the front porch. With a blanket already out there, the two of them sat on a swing, covering up with it in the brisk December night. The electricity of his touch stretched down the side of her as she settled against him.

Part of her mind still held on to the look on his face when she'd said she would marry him just moments before, while the rest of her wanted this moment to last forever.

"Have you enjoyed this trip?" he asked, his voice vibrating against the top of her head.

"Of course. It's my first trip to America, and even though we saw a lot of places in the last two weeks, I think my favorite part is meeting the Montgomerys and reliving the memories you have of Hawthorne. Seeing that the person you are today was molded during your time here."

He tipped her head back with his fingers and kissed her with light kisses.

She pulled back and smiled, leaning her forehead on his.

"I don't know if I'm ready to go back just yet. This has seemed so magical."

"What if you go back as the future Mrs. Roman Hamilton?" The look on his face was somber, almost nervous.

Isabelle sat back, studying his face. "What do you mean?" The words slipped out, even though she understood most of what he'd asked her.

The blanket slipped from around him as he sank to one knee before her. "I originally went looking for a fake ring for you to wear around the Guilberts, but the more I got to know you, the more I wanted it to be a real ring." He opened a small black velvet box and asked, "Isabelle Madeline Rousseau, will you marry me?"

Tears sprang to her eyes, and she nodded, biting her upper lip as she reached for him, wrapping her arms around his neck and pulling him in for a kiss.

"Of course, I'll marry you. You are the one who holds my heart."

"And you mine," he said, slipping the ring onto the appropriate finger. The diamond was large, set with several smaller diamonds in an infinity shape. "It's an Everlon Knot, meant to signify that love never stops."

After kissing him again, she said, "Sounds about right."

He drew her in then, kissing her long and then changing to feather-light kisses along her lips.

"Thank you for loving all of me, even the beastly parts."

* * *

Keep reading for a sneak peek of Evan and Sadie's story in
The Vegas Billionaire.

* * *

Thank you for reading *The British Billionaire!* If you enjoyed it, I would love to see a review from you. You can also subscribe to Britney's newsletter here:
Subscribe to Britney's List

CHAPTER 1

THE VEGAS BILLIONAIRE

Walking out of the large gym on the lower floor of his resort hotel, Evan Pearson wiped his forehead with a towel and walked toward the smoothie counter. With the remodel of several large rooms on the ground floor, he had more fires to put out than normal. The fact that he'd had to run some of the tension off during lunch wasn't a good sign for how the day was going and he could feel the beginnings of a headache just behind his eyes.

"The usual, Cory," he said, slipping onto the stool next to the counter. The lanky college kid behind the counter nodded and pulled out several ingredients, pouring them into the large blender. A lot of people had balked at the idea of a section dedicated to smoothies and flavored drinks would be worth it in his large hotel, but it was one of the highest earning stores throughout his resort.

"How are things today, Mr. Pearson," Cory asked over the sound of the blender.

Wiping his face once more with this towel, Evan said, "Another day at the office. How goes college? You're a business major, right?"

The young man nodded and smiled. "It's harder than I thought it would be."

Grinning, Evan nodded, remembering his time as a student at Hawthorne. It had been seven years since graduation but he could still remember a lot of his teachers and their advice through the four years he was there. "If you ever need help with it, or choosing a future career, come see me. I had some great people help me out in my life and I like to return the favor."

His mind turned to Dan Montgomery, one of the coaches of the football team and house mentor to his fraternity, Delta Phi. The wisdom Dan had shared throughout the years was beyond his years and Evan would always be grateful for it. Since his passing at the beginning of the year, Evan had thought about him even more, grateful to have his voice in Evan's head.

"I'd love that, sir. Business is so broad and I don't want to be trying to pay off loans when I'm fifty." Cory grinned and his comment made Evan throw back his head and laugh.

Cory handed the Styrofoam cup filled with a chocolate protein smoothie and a straw across the counter and nodded, looking at a woman who'd just walked in. "What can I get you?"

"Can I get a strawberry smoothie with a shot of protein in it?" The woman's voice was familiar and Evan spun to look back.

"Taryn?"

She turned, flashing him a smile. "Hey, little brother. Brent told me I'd find you here."

Evan took a sip of his smoothie as he waited for his older sister by two years to pay. She walked over to stand by him and grinned.

"What brings you to Vegas? I thought you were back in California planning your wedding."

Taryn whipped her long ponytail around and rolled her eyes. "I'm here for FitCon. It starts tomorrow but I thought I'd stop by and say hi before I get checked into my hotel."

Raising his eyebrows, he asked, "Why aren't you staying here? You could for free, you know."

With cheesy grin, Taryn said, "I know, but this was just easier because then I don't have to go further than across the street from the convention center to the hotel. After these long days, it will be hard enough to make it to my room before I fall asleep." Taryn had become a health and fitness nut a few years before and worked to share tips and tricks to getting or staying healthy with her followers on Quickstagram, the app Evan's triplet brother, Aiden, had designed.

"How's Travis? Is he almost done with his rotations?" Evan took another sip and waited for the answer as Taryn walked to grab her smoothie and rejoin him.

"He's really good. I'll fly back to California at the end of the week and he'll be back then for a few weeks before the wedding. Speaking of," she said, jutting out her bottom lip and giving him sad eyes, "I need to ask you a favor."

"Okay." Evan felt his stomach clench as he waited for her question. Taryn had always asked some of the hardest questions and he just hoped it wouldn't be dangerous this time.

She took a long sip of her smoothie and he felt his irritation rise. It had to be something big for her to wait this long. Turning, she moved to sit down at a table.

When he slid in on the chair opposite her, she asked, "Would you mind if we use the convention room for our wedding?"

Frowning, Evan said, "What about the 'amazing place' you had booked in California? I thought that was all set."

She bit her upper lip and he could see the emotion playing in her eyes. When she spoke, her voice sounded a bit wobbly, as if she could break into tears at any moment. "Our wedding planner skipped town with our deposit and all the extra money we'd put towards the rentals. We've filed all the paperwork to get it back but if they can't find her, it will be no use. She never booked the venue, caterers or anything, so I'm here stuck at square one, trying to get things figured out on a smaller budget. My wedding is in six weeks and I'm kind of freaking out a bit."

"You're still getting married before Thanksgiving?" he asked. When she nodded, he said, "I'm not sure it will be completely done by then. I've been working on that remodel for a few months and they're just barely getting all the finish work for it."

"Six weeks will be enough time. All you need to do is paint, right?"

Evan shook his head. Only his sister would think it was as easy to just snap his fingers to get things done. With all of the work in the connecting rooms, it could take over a month to paint the entire section and as it was, he needed to find a painter. His other one had moved to Arizona to be closer to his wife's parents and Evan had struggled to find someone consistent enough to do the job.

"I'll see what I can do. If it's not done, we'll just have it in the courtyard. I'm sure the fountain would look great in your pictures."

Taryn pushed his shoulder and frowned. "In November? I know this is Vegas but it's still colder than in the fall. Just promise me you'll try to get the room done? It will help us so much to have things figured out."

"Are you doing all the planning yourself now?"

She shook her head. "No, I've asked Sadie Gibson to help. She's a wedding planner and Aubrey vouched for her skills. She was featured in one of the wedding magazines a few months back so I'd say I'm in good hands. I just wish I'd known that from the start."

Evan tried to think about the red-headed girl who'd been attached at the hip with his triplet sister since they were young. She'd gone to high school with Evan, Aubrey, and Aiden, and had been around for many of the same parties. What would she be like now?

Sadie and Aubrey had been roommates in college but it had been some time since he'd seen her, graduation was probably the last. She'd always been nice but he'd been the big shot football player and had moved in different circles throughout college. Not much time to remember one of his hometown girls.

"Is that what Sadie does now? Plan weddings?" Evan looked at Taryn for confirmation.

"She's a pretty famous one. But you've avoided everything about weddings for the past two years so I can understand why you wouldn't know that." Taryn shifted her purse on her arm and said, "She just got done with Maleah Strong's wedding two weeks ago and it was a vision. I can only hope she can do something like that for our wedding."

Taryn took another sip of her drink and looked up at him. "What about your dating life? Have you been out with anyone lately?"

"You do know I work an insane amount of hours a week and then have to travel often to check on my other hotels. I'm not sure a woman would appreciate a relationship like that."

"I know it still hurts, Evan. But Stacey leaving you at the altar shouldn't be the end of your dating life. You need to get out there and keep trying. You'll find a girl."

Evan threw back his head and laughed. "Right, because running resort hotels is a side job. I just need to get through these remodels with my sanity and then maybe I'll think about dating. But don't think since you'll be happily married that you can set me up over and over with the first girl you find out is single."

Feigning hurt, Taryn said, "I'm the best matchmaker there is, you're just too picky."

"No, Taryn, you're the best fitness blogger I've ever seen but cupid you are not."

Taryn scrunched her nose at him and pulled her purse up over her shoulder. "Just wait. I'll make sure you find someone amazing and she'll make sure to put you in your place, Mr. Billionaire." She winked at him and said, "I've got to head over. I'm supposed to help set up the registration table."

She leaned in and gave him a hug. "You'll be fine, Ev. Just don't close yourself off completely to love."

When they pulled apart, Evan said, "Tell Travis hi for me."

Taryn nodded and disappeared through the door and Evan walked over to the elevator. When it opened, he pushed the button for the penthouse and swiped his card to allow the elevator to grant the request. Leaning back against the wall of the elevator, Evan knew he needed to make a few calls and get things lined up to make his sister's new wedding dreams come true.

TO KEEP READING, check out *The Vegas Billionaire.*

ACKNOWLEDGMENTS

Thank you so much for reading this book! I hope you enjoyed it and make sure to leave a review!

You, the reader, are the one I think about as I work through these novels and thank you for continuing to support me. Starting a new series gets a little scary because it's new and I just hope you love these characters as much as I have.

To Karen O'Connor and Rebecca Andrew who helped transform Roman into a true Brit. Thank you so much for your help with all the little fixes and for your time reading through this book!

Thank you, Max, for taking the kids every Thursday so I can pour my heart out on the page. I'm a better mother and a more sane wife when I have those small breaks.

Julie L. Spencer, Elizabeth McCay, Shannon Symonds and Deborah Goodman. Some of the best and funnest romance people I could associate with. I love our Thursday night chats and the late hours talking about whatever is going on in our lives. The long Facebook threads and the fun laughter as we work through our bad first drafts down to the final edits.

To Christina Schrunk for her patience in working with me on these books. Her ideas and insight help to spark those last final puzzle pieces to help the book come together and I am so grateful for her.

To Krista Burdine for proofreading this book. She keeps me sane so I don't have to reread the book 100 times before publishing to hopefully get all of the errors out.

If you want news on when the next book comes out or my progress on the series, make sure to subscribe to the list so you don't miss anything.

We are grateful for readers like you and can't wait for you to enjoy the next book!

ABOUT THE AUTHOR

Britney Mills was born in Utah but parts of her heart lie in Boston, Washington D.C. and Germany. Her love of writing began with the third grade book her teacher assigned her to write and she spent hours hidden behind her mother's couch writing pages and pages about knights and castles. Now she writes about romance. Go figure.

When she's not mothering her four small children, writing or reading, she's probably out playing a sport, going on a hike, or binge watching a murder mystery series. The way to her heart is through homemade chocolate chip cookies and five minutes peace.

www.ingramcontent.com/pod-product-compliance
Lightning Source LLC
Chambersburg PA
CBHW021330190726
48288CB00003B/1046